Beneath Venomous Sails

·Book One·

H. M. Huntress

Beneath Venomous Sails is a spin-off/continuation of the Forbidden Waves duology and world. Though it can be read separately, there will be spoilers for the Forbidden Waves books.

For anyone wishing they could run away with pirates rather than deal with real life...

Here is a Spotify playlist of songs
which remind me of *Beneath Venomous Sails*!
*Please note this playlist is subject
to change at any time*

Scan the QR code with the camera
on your phone to listen now!

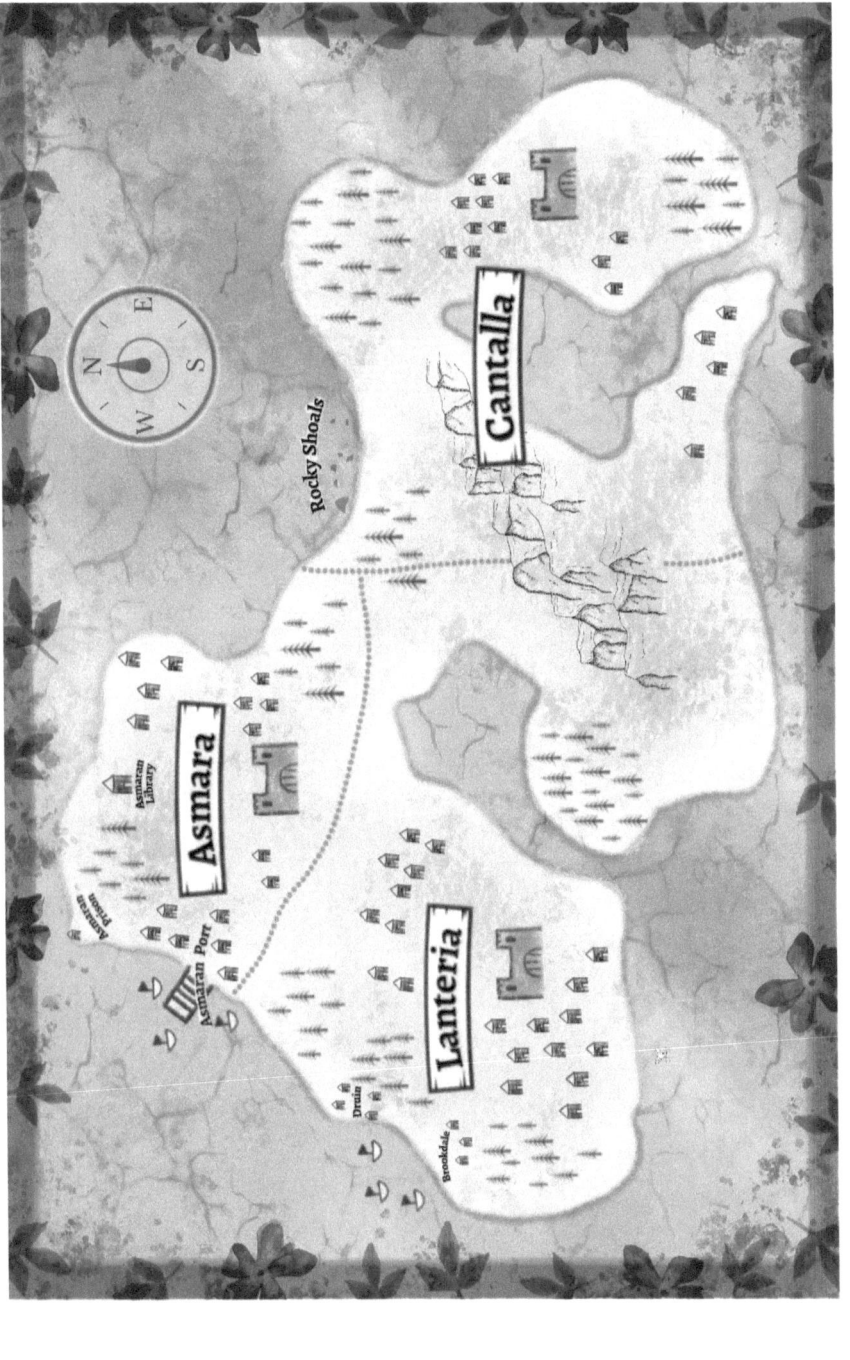

Nora

The sea goddess, Neros, herself couldn't bring me down as I cut through the water, chasing after Lia. It had been a dream spending the last two years underwater, living in Thalassia, but my time there was coming to an end.

Lia and my parents agreed I could stay as long as I wanted, but it didn't call to me quite like being on land did. True, I enjoyed it immensely, but I couldn't shake the feeling that I was missing something. So, tomorrow I would return home.

Sometimes I almost felt like I was playing mermaids, rather than actually *being* one. Like it was all a fantasy that I'd created in my mind, and reality was about to crash back in on me.

I'm going to miss this! Lia said in my mind. *You need to come visit more often.*

Smiling, I kept my mouth shut so water wouldn't try to rush in. *I'll miss this, too.* I responded.

I'd never get used to the telepathy of mermaids while underwater. It seemed a little invasive to me, but it was the only

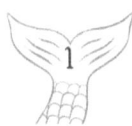

way to communicate unless we went above water every time we had something to say.

Lia stopped short, almost making me run into her, and when I was only inches away, she pulled me in for a hug. I laughed, knowing she wouldn't hear it, and a stream of bubbles escaped.

Come on. Your mom should be arriving soon, Lia said.

My mom had insisted on coming to Thalassia to bring me home, though I was twenty-three and perfectly capable of making the trip home alone. She said she wanted to visit with some old friends, but I knew how much she disliked her old home. The only reason she was coming was because she didn't trust me not to get into trouble. Not that I ever had, but for some reason, she and my father were convinced that the second I was left alone someone would sweep in and steal me away from them.

Lia took my hand as we swam through the underwater civilization that was Thalassia. Some of the structures were made entirely of shells, big and small, while others were built into existing caves and rocks. The castle where Lia lived was built into a rock formation, but what wasn't made from nature was either made of glass or gold. All the doorways were made of gold. There weren't any actual doors, which was something to get used to.

All the merpeople that we passed waved to Lia. She was their queen, after all. I couldn't imagine shouldering that kind of responsibility, but she handled it with more grace than I could ever see myself managing. My parents wouldn't even let me out of the house without an escort, I hardly had the experience to become a leader of any sort.

Scowling, I stared down at the ocean floor.

What's going through your head? Lia asked, and I turned to find her watching me carefully.

We stopped as we swam into the entryway of the castle.

I considered lying to Lia and telling her I was fine, but she'd always been the more understanding one out of my entire family.

I love and miss Mom and Dad, I do. But I'm not looking forward to going home and losing what semblance of freedom I've had while I've been here, I told her.

Understanding softened Lia's features. *Your parents love you so much,* she said, which I knew. *And I know they've been a bit ... overprotective. But them letting you come here was a big step for them! I truly believe they might finally see some sense and realize you're a grown woman and can take care of yourself, for the most part.* She winked and laughed, the bubbles streaming up between us.

It was only a few short hours ago I'd gotten lost on our outing and had to reach out to Lia to help navigate back to her. That could easily be blamed on the fact that most of the ocean looked the same, though. Not my lack of navigation skills.

I hope you're right, I said. *I'm going to go grab a few things from my room before mom comes.*

In my room, I really didn't have much, but I needed a second alone. I sat on my bed and imagined the adventures I might have once my parents allowed me to go out on my own. Maybe I'd make some friends outside of my parents' world and be able to find a place that truly felt like home. As much as I loved my family, I'd begun to feel out of place living in the

middle of nowhere. We were too far away from most towns to be able to visit frequently and make friends there.

I knew my parents had picked that location on purpose. It was safer, farther away from other people.

Your mother is here. Lia's voice popped into my head.

At least she gave me a warning before my mother's voice came into the mix out of nowhere.

I'm coming in, I missed you too much to wait for you to come out. Viv's words followed shortly after Lia's. And as she forewarned, she swam through the entryway into my room and threw her arms around me.

I missed you too, I told her. Even if I wanted to escape from being under my parents' thumb, it didn't mean that I didn't miss them when I was apart from them. I still loved them, and knew they'd only kept me sheltered all these years because they loved me and worried about me.

Lia told me you went and visited The Leona's wreck last week. Viv smoothed a hand over my hair, which I kept braided when underwater. Otherwise, it went a little wild when I wasn't moving.

I gripped the end of my braid and tugged it lightly. Both my parents had brown hair, so it was inevitable I would too. But I'd inherited my father's stormy gray eyes. I envied my mother's golden eyes, because they stood out so much more starkly than my own.

I finally believe that Dad may have been a pirate in a past life, I teased. The Leona had been my dad, Finn's ship back when he'd been a pirate captain. He'd told stories about his time spent as a pirate, but I could never really picture it. Even when we'd visited Jami on his ship, who had taken over as

4

captain once Finn stepped down, and Finn stood behind the helm, it just didn't match with the man I knew. Especially not the stories our family friend Marley told. I refused to believe those.

Viv smiled. *Your dad will be so happy to hear you say that. All he wants is for you and your sister to know how bad ass he used to be.* Her mouth parted slightly, and I knew she was laughing. I wished I could hear it under the water, because I missed her laugh.

As much as I wanted to leave home, I knew it would be crushing at the same time to be apart from them again so soon. At least while I'd been in Thalassia my mom would come visit every few weeks, and I went home for big events and holidays. Though, spending my first Celebration of Neros under the sea had been quite the experience. I'd decided there was no other way to spend the day in the future.

The day of thanks was coming up in a few days, when all my parent's friends would gather at our house and give thanks to all the gods. Dad always made sure we remembered he didn't believe in any gods, other than my mother. Apparently, she was a sea goddess in his eyes and anytime he reminded us of that I simultaneously swooned and cringed.

I figured after seeing all their friends it would be the perfect time to ask my parents if I could do some traveling on my own. They'd be in a great mood, and they wouldn't even care that their first-born daughter was about to leave them for who knew how long.

It sounded a lot worse when I put it like that. I wouldn't say it like that to them. *Noted,* I thought to myself.

Talking into Viv's mind, I said, *I wish Dad could come to Thalassia. Didn't Uncle Jami make the trip once?* I could have sworn I'd heard him tell a story of some wild magic Lia had managed to convince a mage to do to allow him to be able to visit Thalassia for a brief time.

Mom rolled her eyes. *Oh, yes. And he'll never let us forget it. He likes to pretend he's an expert on all things Thalassia now.*

Lia's presence pressed into my mind. A lot of times she didn't bother to let me know she was about to speak telepathically, but she had the courtesy to do it when I was talking with someone else.

Shall we get going? she asked, appearing in my bedroom's entryway.

Once we were back on land, my ears popped, and sound rushed back in. It was always a shocking experience to go from being underwater for so long to back on land. Everything seemed so jarring after spending so much time with the muted sounds of ocean life.

"Jami hasn't arrived at the house yet," Viv said to Lia once we were all dried off and fully clothed.

I didn't have any fancy jewelry like them yet that allowed my clothes to shift with me. So, I had to bring a bag with me if I was planning on shifting and then remove the excess water with the little magic I had outside of my mer form. It was much harder to come by those kinds of magical items than it had been when my parents got theirs.

"I don't know what you're talking about," Lia said. She twisted her bright green hair up into a bun, securing it with a

6

gold pick. "I was getting sick of Thalassia and needed to get away is all."

Mom shot me a look and we both smiled. Lia was terrible at hiding her longing for Jami. In the two years I'd spent with her, she'd only seen him on the holidays we visited my home. All my life, he'd never missed a formal gathering, and sulked when Lia didn't show up. They were both insufferable when it came to their relationship.

But at least they had one. I'd never been in love. There had been a few times I'd sneaked away for a few hours when we visited towns and danced with or kissed boys, but then we had to leave. It was quite an unspectacular love life. I'd met a man in Thalassia, Marc, who held some promise, but he wanted to stay in Thalassia. So, I knew we'd never work. I hadn't even bothered to say goodbye. At least we had fun together for a while.

I wanted a love like Jami and Lia's, or my parents'. Or Marley and Nix's.

"Hey," Lia murmured, brushing my shoulder with her own. "I know that look."

Viv glanced back at us, still on the sand while she hopped onto her horse as if she hadn't heard Lia, but I knew she was listening.

Even though Lia hadn't been planning on joining us, Viv had still known to bring a horse for her. They were scary sometimes with how well they knew each other.

Lia continued, "You'll find your person someday. Or people." She smirked. "There's no rules saying you have to choose just one."

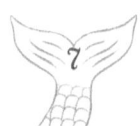

I giggled. "I appreciate the encouragement, but I think I'm a one-person kinda gal."

Viv laughed, confirming my suspicion of her listening in, and her horse veered onto the dirt road, trotting away.

Lia and I each mounted our own horses and followed her.

"It's hard to meet people when I'm always with someone. Either my parents, my sister, or *you*," I said, giving Lia a knowing look.

Winking, Lia nodded and cleared her throat. "It's almost like maybe your parents should loosen their reins a little on you. You're newly twenty-three and ready to take on the world."

Viv didn't even bother to pretend she wasn't listening anymore. "There are a lot of dangerous people in the world. And you have hundreds of years to figure out your life and fall in love."

"So, we think," I muttered, casting my gaze to the side. The dirt kicked up around our horses' hooves, but I could see little purple flowers growing along the road. "I may have inherited Dad's human lifespan."

Viv sighed, shaking her head. "That's not how it works. You're a mermaid shifter, and so you'll live a mermaid's longer lifespan."

"Well," Lia interjected. "We can't know for sure. She is the first child ever born to two different shifters."

A fact that I was simultaneously proud of and terrified of. It meant there was so much left up to chance and the unknown. Would I live a normal human lifespan, or hundreds of years like a mermaid? Would I present with two shifting

abilities, or only as a mermaid? At twenty-three, it was highly unlikely I'd also be a lion shifter, but as we knew, we knew *nothing*.

"Let's talk about something else, please," Viv snapped. Whenever the topic of my lifespan came up, she panicked, which was fair. She didn't want to outlive her children *and* her husband. A lump formed in my throat as it always did when I thought about the prospect of living *hundreds* of years without my father.

I took a deep breath and refocused on my surroundings. Clouds were rolling in from the North behind us and it looked like it might rain. We always came in from the water at the northernmost point of Asmara because it was closer to our house. That and my parents avoided the Asmaran port as much as possible, which was why I'd chosen it as my first stop when I could finally leave on my solo journey.

Apparently, Finn had a lot of enemies from his time as a pirate, but since I didn't entirely believe he'd ever been one, I assumed most of those enemies were made up as well. That didn't mean I'd be careless, though. My parents taught me how to wield a sword, and my claws.

It was dark, and the rain had started by the time we reached home. Ample food was waiting for us on the dining room table, and a warm hug from my dad soothed the rest of my worries for the time being.

"Your sister helped me with the food," Finn said, waving a hand over the roast and potatoes. We all took seats and filled our plates.

As if summoned by Finn's mention of her, the creaking of floorboards announced Bree's arrival in the dining room, and she skipped in from the hall.

"Nora!" She swooped down and hugged me. All I could do from my awkward angle was pat her shoulder.

"I missed you too, Bree." I chuckled. "Let me eat though. It's been too long since I've had something other than fish."

Eating under the sea had been hard to grow accustomed to. It was a lot of uncooked fish, seaweed, and other seafood that never quite had enough variety of flavors. There was *always* too much salt.

Bree dropped into the seat beside mine and propped her elbow on the table.

"Tell me everything," she demanded. "What was it like? Did you have any adventures? Meet any cool people? *Boys?*" She waggled her eyebrows at that last one.

Instead of answering, I continued to eat.

"We had a lot of fun, didn't we, Nora?" Lia said. "We visited the only other undersea kingdom, Neria, in the south, then we headed to Sylvane to check out where your dad and Jami grew up."

Bree perked up. "I've always wanted to go there! Can we go when I come to stay with you next year?"

"Of course!" Lia grinned.

My mind snagged on something she'd said. "Next year?" I asked. "But you'll only be eighteen, I had to wait until I was twenty-one." A stab of annoyance struck me, dissolving my appetite.

Finn cleared his throat and stared across the table at Viv, who bit her lip.

"But you proved it's safe for us, so now I can go," Bree said warily. "Right, Mom?" Her gaze darted to Viv's.

"Exactly," Viv said. "We only made you wait longer, Nora, because Lia wasn't ready to take you in yet."

Lia's eyes widened and she sucked in her cheeks. I could tell she was biting her tongue so as not to cause any more trouble, which only made me more upset.

They were lying to me.

I slammed my hands on the table and stood, nearly knocking my chair over.

"I have *always* had to wait longer than Bree to do anything. And she has more freedom than I ever had!" I kept my gaze on the table, unable to find the courage to look at my parents as I went on. "My first solo trip to the library was at fifteen, Bree's was at twelve." I lifted a finger and then another as I added, "You wouldn't let me leave the house alone until I was ten, and Bree immediately got that privilege after I did."

"Nora." Viv pushed her chair back and came over to me, putting a hand on my shoulder. I shook it off.

"I'm done living like this," I cut her off. "I can't do it anymore. I—" The words stuck in my throat, and I stormed out of the room. I hadn't thrown a tantrum like that in a long time, but it felt very freeing, even if it was embarrassing.

My bedroom upstairs was the same as I had left it. Once Finn's younger siblings, Tabby and the twins, Leo and Atty, had moved out, I was finally able to have my own room, and I cherished it. It was the only place I was able to be truly alone.

11

Books were stacked in the far corner beside my bed, while my wardrobe stood right next to the door, with more books piled atop it. Since I wasn't able to live out my own adventures, I'd been forced to live vicariously through those books. Most of them had been given to me by Shannon, one of the witches in the Asmaran library. Every few years they had to get rid of books to make room for new ones, and she always offered them to us first.

Curling up on my bed, I closed my eyes and tried to imagine myself living as a queen in another land, able to do whatever I pleased.

Before I could get far, someone knocked on my door.

"Come in," I grumbled.

Finn stepped into my room and closed the door behind him. I'd expected my mom, or even Bree, so I sat up and stared at him in surprise.

He sighed and gave me a half smile.

"Can I sit?" he asked, waving to the bed.

I nodded and he sat beside me, making the bed dip under his weight and jostling me.

"I understand why you're upset, and you're right to be. Your mother and I have been unfair, and we haven't been honest with you about a lot of things." He ran a hand through his hair, and I could tell this was hard for him to talk about. So, I said nothing and let him find his words, as he and my mom had always done for me whenever I needed to talk to them about things.

"As difficult as it's been for you to believe, I *did* used to be a pirate captain," he teased, nudging me with his elbow. We

both laughed, but he stopped sooner, and his smile faded. "And with that position, I created a lot of enemies."

"I know," I said. "You and Mom told me."

He shook his head. "It's not only that, though. We left out that I used to work for King Danforth—"

"What?" I gasped. "You worked for the *king?*"

"Yes. But the things I had to do for him made me even more enemies than being Captain Finn ever did. Including the king himself."

"Oh," I huffed. "Then why didn't you leave Asmara?"

"We considered it, but when we came here and saw this house, we fell in love. And having the witches so close at the library, made your mother feel better about raising a family here," he explained. "We always thought that someday we might go to Sylvane, and we still may, but this was our easiest option at the time. And we haven't regretted it."

"But why have you been so much stricter with me than Bree?" I asked.

"That is a little more complicated, and you have to promise not to tell your sister, because we love you both equally," he said, pointing a finger at me.

"Yeah, yeah, okay," I agreed, laughing. "We all know I'm the favorite but go on."

"We never knew, never *know,* I guess, what's coming with you. We didn't know how long it would take for you to shift for the first time, and we didn't know if you'd be a lion shifter, or a mermaid shifter, or somehow both. We still don't know what the future holds for you, and we don't know how people will react to finding out who you are. The first child born to two different shifters, *ever.*" He took my hand. "You have paved the

way for your sister, and I'm sorry that it took a little longer for your mother and I to be comfortable enough to give you some freedom. It's not that we love you or your sister any differently, but you were our first, and we held on a bit too tightly I guess."

"I forgive you for loving me too much and clearly playing favorites," I said, sticking my tongue out at him and making him laugh.

Sometimes it was hard to be this close to him, when I could see all the signs of aging that Viv wouldn't show for another hundred years or so. The streaks of gray in his hair and beard, and the wrinkles beside his eyes and mouth.

"I love you, Dad." I leaned in against him and he put his arm around my shoulders. "But I need to be able to live my life, without you, or mom, or Aunt Lia watching over my shoulder."

His shoulders rose and fell with his sigh. "I know. How about we talk about it after the celebration? Once things calm down and we can discuss logistics, and safety, and—"

"Really?" I grinned and pulled back to look up at him. "I promise I'll do whatever you and mom want, so long as I can go do *something* on my own." I put my hands together and gave him my best pleading eyes.

Ruffling my hair, he stood and stepped away from the bed, making me feel like I was a teenager rather than about to turn twenty-three. "Like I said, we'll talk *after* the celebration. Deal?"

"Deal!" I squealed with joy.

Adrian

Time and again my father warned me about the men who would try to use me to get to him, and time and again I ignored him and took risks I shouldn't. Granted, I could hold my own against ten or so men, but not when I was drunk off my ass and barely able to stand.

So, that night, I got a little more banged up than usual.

My father also warned me that though others thought I was a weak spot for him, he'd never actually give anything up, or comply with any demands just to get me back. He didn't care about me *that* much. The only reason he kept me around was because I was a good fighter, and a powerful shifter. Well, that and he had use for my venom.

"This is a bad idea," one of the men whispered behind me where I was tied up in a chair, probably looking pathetic. "The captain will kill us all."

Another man scoffed. "That's if he catches us. We'll be long gone as soon as we get the money."

I couldn't help but laugh, which made them all stop talking. Unlike them, I knew my time would come. As soon as I

sobered up enough for the room to stop spinning and to focus long enough to shift and escape my binds. I also wanted to give them a little bit of hope that they might get that money before murdering them all for daring to come after *me.*

I scowled as I realized how much I sounded like my father in my own head.

"Word has been sent." Another man entered the basement. I had no idea where they were coming from because it was behind me, and I'd been unconscious when I'd been drug in there. Polly kept warning me not to keep getting into fights, and *maybe* I'd start listening to her after this.

"So, you three should get lost." The first man spoke again. "The less here when the captain arrives, the better. He's not a shifter, so he shouldn't be able to sense us, but I'm not taking any chances."

He's not a shifter. No. My father wasn't. The shifter gene had skipped a generation, as it often did when non-shifter genes were introduced to a bloodline. He had snake shifter in his genes for me to come into existence, but my mother had been the shifter. She'd promptly dropped me on my father's doorstep, or more accurately ship deck, as soon as I turned eight and shifted for the first time. Apparently, she couldn't handle dealing with a son who could shift when she could barely manage taking care of herself.

"It's not him you should be worrying about," I said, finding my voice, though it came out hoarse and low.

Someone snickered behind me. "He's awake after all."

I ran my tongue over my top teeth, ensuring my snake fangs were extended. Sometimes when I got too drunk, they

16

came out without prompting. This time, I'd kept them under control, but they were needed now.

"If you let me go, I'll give you what I have inside my coat pocket," I offered, knowing that my pockets were empty. I'd spent every coin I had in the tavern. The one thing I had of any value was a leather bracelet wrapped around my wrist, and it only held value to myself. It had been my mother's and either she left it for me when she ditched me, or she dropped it running away, but I kept it. Her name, *Elise,* was etched into it alongside a rose.

"We'd rather wait and see what haul your father brings in trade for you," a too-smug voice said.

"That's a shame," I sighed.

A man strolled into view, stopping in front of me and sneering at me. "But that won't stop me from taking what you have anyway."

As I'd expected, he reached for my jacket and I lunged forward, as much as my binds would allow, and bit down hard on his bicep. Yelping in pain, he leapt back, ripping my fangs from his arm and leaving two gashes behind.

"I would either get to a mage or a healer as fast as you can, or else ... Well." I tutted.

He turned ghostly pale and stared down at his arm in shock. Movement behind me told me that multiple guns and swords were pointed my way.

Shifting always brought with it some discomfort, but it also gave me a sense of belonging. I knew who I was when I shifted into my snake form, and I knew who to kill.

The ropes that had bound me dropped to the floor, useless. I had to get used to the colors changing to two primary

colors, blue and green, but otherwise, my body knew exactly how to move and exist in my snake form. I was as long as I'd been tall in my human form, and completely black. So, I blended in with the dark floor of the basement.

The men, who I could now see stood by an open door, ran up the stairs leading out into the night. They knew better than to attempt to deal with a shifter with bullets. The swords might be a bit more effective, but I never let anyone close enough to use one against me in this form. The man who I'd bitten ran past me and I shifted back into my human form. It was easier to fight as a human.

I picked up a sword someone had dropped and threw it, pommel over blade, with precise aim, lodging it in the guy's back. Even from behind, I could see where it protruded out of his chest. He collapsed and I wrenched the sword from his corpse on my way out the door.

After shifting, most of the lingering effects of alcohol had disappeared thanks to the benefit of healing faster in my shifted form. That and the adrenaline kicking in.

Much to my dismay, by the time I made it up the stairs into the alley, everyone else had scattered. I wouldn't be killing anyone else that night.

Footsteps crunched in the gravel ahead of me and a shadow moved toward me. I raised my sword, ready to fight.

"Captain Kerrigan is waiting for you." It was Morgan, my father's first mate. She always referred to my father as *Captain Kerrigan,* as if he deserved the deference she showed him. She was unfazed by my raised weapon and glanced at it, brow raised. "You're not bringing that on board."

Turning on her heel, she stuck her hands in her coat pockets and strode away, expecting me to follow. So, I did.

Dropping the sword, I walked behind her as if I were a dog on a leash. Kerrigan may have made the rules and demanded they be followed, but Morgan was the one who doled out the punishments if anyone stepped out of line, until she taught me to do it and turned me into an enemy of most of the crew. She'd also been the one who raised me once my mother abandoned me. So, we had a complicated relationship.

We walked across the docks, which were still busy with people going from bar to bar or between ships.

"Would you have saved me if I hadn't escaped?" I asked Morgan. Her hat shadowed most of her face, but I saw her lips twitch, almost as if she might smile.

But she never smiled.

"I knew you'd escape," she said.

So, *no.* I shrugged. It wasn't as if I ever expected anyone to come to my rescue. Ever since I was dropped onto my father's ship, I knew I'd have to be the one to save myself. Every. Single. Time. And I did. Anytime anyone else got into a fight, I was the first to sit back and watch. If no one wanted to help me, that was fine, but they sure as shit shouldn't expect me to help them.

We reached the gangplank leading up to our ship, *Wave Breaker.* When I was ten, I told my father it was a lame name, and he threw something at me that gave me a scar beside my left eye. I couldn't remember what he threw, but I think it was his spyglass. Sometimes I caught myself rubbing the scar when I was deep in thought, and I cursed him.

Being both the most feared and the wealthiest pirate of the moment, my father's ship was larger than any other in the port. Being King Danforth's bitch had its perks.

Morgan led the way to Kerrigan's quarters, as if I could get lost on the ship. His quarters took up the whole of the back of the main deck. One level beneath it were mine and Morgan's quarters. We each had our own room, though they were only big enough for the beds and a wash bucket.

The crew slept in one large area outside of mine and Morgan's rooms. You could hear all of them snoring through the thin, plank-made walls.

In his quarters, Kerrigan sat at his desk, writing something on what looked like a poster. As we got closer, I saw the big letters at the top, *'Wanted.'*

"Who's that for?" I asked, but he didn't even bother to lift his head.

"Killed one from Bart's crew this time," Morgan said, dropping into a chair in front of the desk. "I already informed Captain Bart of the situation."

My lip curled as I glanced over at her and sat in the chair beside hers. "How?"

"Don't question her," Kerrigan snapped. "You're the one who started this whole mess."

I scoffed. "I was *captured* and *bound.* How is this my fault?"

Kerrigan lifted his head and looked at me. "You always start these things. None of my other crew members seem to have as much trouble as you."

It was true, I did tend to run my mouth once I'd had a few drinks, and start a few fights, but it wasn't like I *wanted* to be

20

taken for ransom. Though I did enjoy fighting my way out most of the time.

"It's done. Now we're moving on to this." Kerrigan held up his poster so I could read it in full.

Wanted
Leonora Harper
Daughter of Finnian and Vivianne Harper
If found, deliver ALIVE to Captain Kerrigan
Known mermaid shifter

"What the fuck is this about?" I asked, glancing between Morgan and Kerrigan. "You want to steal some kid?"

The annoyance was almost palpable as Kerrigan returned his focus to me.

"First, no more speaking unless you are spoken to. Second, she is not *some child*, she is the first child to ever have been born to two different shifters. Do you understand the amount of gold someone will pay to have her and try to find a way to allow more interbreeding?" Kerrigan leaned across the desk, the poster lowered to his side. The way he spoke of shifters like animals set my teeth on edge. "And, if her father comes to try and save her, I can finally take my revenge."

I put my hands up as if surrendering. "Right, sorry. Carry on." From the name on the poster, *Finnian,* I assumed it was the same Captain Finn who had slighted my father years prior, before I'd ever come into his life. He certainly knew how to hold a grudge.

Kerrigan leaned back and snapped his fingers at Morgan. "Get him out. I can't deal with him right now."

I stood before Morgan could take my arm and force me up. "I can leave on my own, I didn't even want to be here."

I considered going back into town and trying to pick another fight, but the night was coming to an end, and I was exhausted.

In bed, I regretted my decision to turn in for the night when I overheard two crew members, Polly and Nate, talking about me.

"When is he going to learn that no matter how many times he's kidnapped, his father is never going to love him," Polly said.

I knew they weren't talking maliciously; they were the only two of my crewmates who seemed to care whenever I went missing, but they weren't stupid. They knew I could avoid being taken and they were right about one thing: my father would never love me. However, I couldn't care less if he ever gave two shits about me. All I cared about was becoming more feared than he ever dreamed of being and taking the only thing he *did* care about away from him: his ship and his title.

Nora

Our family and friends all arrived the next morning.

After spending a few moments alone with Lia, Jami took Finn aside and had a very serious look on his face.

"What do you think that's about?" I asked Marley, who sat beside me at the dining room table. Everyone had scattered around the house, but I tried to stay near Marley because she had the best stories, and I needed some inspiration for my upcoming excursion into the real world.

"Well, I shouldn't tell you, but since it's about *you,*" Marley started, glancing around to make sure no one else was listening. "How much have your parents told you about Marcus Humer?"

"Well, I know what he did to Mom, and how he made it so she could have children with Dad, using magic." Fear gnawed at my stomach at the thought that this was a pertinent topic again. "Why?"

"Nix and I met up with your Uncle Jami in the port for a few drinks before we came here, and we were quite surprised to hear someone talking about *you.*" Marley sucked her bottom

lip between her teeth and clasped her hands in front of her on the table. "They were talking about how much you might be worth to someone out there, similar to Humer, who would use you to figure out how more people can become like your mom."

"Why me? Why not Mom?" I gasped as I realized what I said. "Not that they should want to take my mom! I just mean ... Why me?" This was going to ruin my plans. My parents would never let me leave Asmara, let alone the house with this news.

I looked at where Finn stood with Jami beside the buffet table. Rage and fear warred on his face. Pushing away from the table, I hurried over to them.

"Dad, please don't let this change your mind about me leaving," I pleaded.

At first his brow furrowed in confusion, but then he glared at Marley. "You had no business telling her," he growled.

"Telling her what?" Viv asked as she entered the room from the kitchen with Lia.

No, no, no, no, no. I tried to give Finn a *'don't tell Mom'* look, but clearly he didn't pick up on the intent.

"I didn't want to ruin the celebration tonight, but I thought you should know," Jami explained. "There's been talk in the port about Leonora and the possibility of using her to replicate what Humer did with you, Viv."

To Viv's credit, she didn't even blink. Humer had been a man who experiments on all kinds of shifters, trying to make it so that shifters could procreate with non-like shifters. Viv had been one of the shifters he experimented on, and one of the few who had survived and been rescued. Though, she was the only one he was successful with, thanks to magic.

Lia spoke first. "I'll kill anyone who tries to take her."

"We knew this day might come," Viv said. "And we've kept her safe this long, so we'll continue to do so."

I panicked, thinking that meant I'd be stuck at home forever. "No!" I cried out, making everyone look at me. "I mean, Dad said he'd consider letting me go off on my own for a while, and I don't want this to change that."

"Of course it changes that," Finn said, throwing his hands in the air. "I can't let you leave knowing that someone's out there waiting to capture you and experiment on you!"

"This is literally my worst nightmare come to life," Viv murmured, running a hand over her short hair.

Lia put her arm around Viv's shoulders. "Nothing's going to happen to Nora. She's smart and resourceful, and she has an entire army of people who will fight to keep her safe."

"This isn't fair! This is my life! I should be able to choose whether I want to risk being captured by some crazy person so that I can actually *live* my life!" Now I was the one who was starting to sound a little crazy. But I couldn't stay there anymore, no matter who was out to get me.

Viv left Lia's side to put her arm around me. "I understand how you're feeling, honey, but—"

"No you don't! You grew up in Thalassia where you had complete freedom once you came of age. And then you traveled the world with Lia and your other friends." I moved away from her. "You don't understand how I'm feeling. I get that you love me and want to protect me, but I can't take this anymore."

Running out of the room, I veered to the front door instead of the stairs. Confining myself to my room would do nothing to staunch the fire burning inside me that needed to

escape. A prickling under my skin told me that my body yearned to shift, so I headed for the lake and dove in.

For the first time, swimming beneath the water in my mer form did nothing to ease the prickling sensation. It didn't take long for Bree to find me.

We swam side by side for a while.

Mom won't tell me what happened, but she said you were upset, she spoke in my mind. *If this is about me going to Thalassia, I can wait a few more years.*

I smiled at that. Bree had always been willing to give up her own happiness for others, but I didn't want her to do that. She deserved her chance at living a life outside of this place. Maybe she'd feel at home in Thalassia, unlike me. Maybe she'd find love there.

No. It's not about that. I'm happy for you and can't wait to hear all your stories. I reassured her.

Then what is this all about? No one will tell me. Her wide eyes, though filled with earnestness, were also innocent.

I'd promised Finn I wouldn't tell her, and I didn't want to scare her with the truth, but I knew if the situation was reversed, I'd want to know. And we'd never kept secrets from each other before. So, I told her everything.

At the end, we climbed out of the lake and sat side by side on the shore.

"So, does that mean people don't know I exist?" Bree asked. It was a good question, but I didn't have an answer.

"I don't know. It might be because I was born first that they want me? Or maybe they have some shred of decency and think you're too young to kidnap? But that seems like an

improbability." Anyone evil enough to experiment on people wouldn't care whether those people were of age or children.

"I'm sorry, Nora. If I could change places with you so you could go explore the world, I would." Wrapping her arm around me she pulled me close and rested her head on my shoulder.

"I know you would," I sighed.

I was embarrassed to walk back up to the house after my outburst. Not because I thought I was wrong, but because of how I handled it. My parents would never take me seriously if I kept running away.

Viv pulled me aside into the sitting room while everyone else went into the dining room where the food for our celebration was waiting. In the hours Bree and I had been gone, everyone had been busy.

"I'm sorry," I said, hanging my head. "I shouldn't have yelled and ran off, but it doesn't change how I feel." I wrapped my arms around myself.

Viv put her hands on my shoulders, and I met her gaze. "No. I'm sorry. We shouldn't have panicked like that. You were right, you deserve to have a say in your life, and knowing the risks makes it a lot easier to avoid them. But that doesn't mean you're going out there by yourself."

I perked up. "But that means I *am* going! Right?"

Viv pursed her lips, hiding her smile, but I caught it. "There are rules," she said. "And you won't be alone, I don't care how old you are. You'll use a fake name, and I want letters every week."

27

I couldn't stop smiling and threw my arms around her. "I promise I'll do whatever you want! Oh my gods, thank Neros."

"Neros has nothing to do with this," Finn said, leaning against the doorframe. "Your mother is very convincing when she wants to be."

I hugged her again, tighter.

Laughing, she hugged me back. "I told you I understand, and I do. We may not have had the same upbringing, but that doesn't mean I don't know what you're searching for." Viv smiled and tucked hair that had slipped out of my braid behind my ear.

"I swear, you are not going to regret this," I said.

"Oh, we already do," Finn joked.

After dinner we discussed the logistics of my departure at the dinner table. Nix won a bet that had been going on for years, guessing when Viv and Finn would finally let me leave the house to go somewhere without them or Lia. Marley had started it, of course.

"You'll go with Jami back to the port," Finn explained. "Marley and Nix will watch out for you from there. You'll use the name Sonora, so you can still have people call you Nora and you won't get confused."

"That was my idea," Nix chimed in from where she leaned against the back wall. "Easiest way to blow your cover is to not respond when someone calls your fake name."

"And you'll avoid pirates as much as possible," Finn said, knocking his fist on the table in finality.

Marley and Lia both burst out laughing.

"As if she can avoid pirates in the pirate hub of the world. The Asmaran port is not the place to visit if you don't want a pirate to cross your path every other minute," Marley said, leaning back in her chair to the point it was almost tipping.

"Marley," I snapped. This was my one chance, and she wasn't helping. "Please, stop talking."

"Right." She winked and put her hand over her mouth.

"If at any point you change your mind and want to come home, there's no shame in that," Finn said, and I could tell he wanted me to bite and say I'd changed my mind. But I held my tongue. No matter how much it scared me to know that there were people out there who wanted to hurt me, it excited me more to finally be going out into the world with people who would let me have some fun.

Marley and Nix were the easiest going in the family, and even though I knew they'd do anything to keep me safe, they'd also be more agreeable to my antics.

"We'll leave in the morning," Jami said. "And my ship is headed to Sylvane if you want to come along with us instead of exploring Asmara."

"I think I'll pass this time," I said. "But thank you."

The rest of the night we played games and enjoyed being together. Bree insisted on sleeping in my room that night, because she said she'd miss me too much and needed as much time with me as possible.

"Knock, knock," Viv said, leaning into the doorway. "Mind if I come in and say goodnight?"

It wasn't something we'd done since I was a teenager, but since I'd be leaving for who knew how long in the morning, I nodded eagerly.

29

Bree squished closer to me while Viv sat on the edge of the bed, placing her hand over the blanket on my knee.

"Tonight has brought up some things that I wanted to talk to the two of you about," she said, a sad smile ghosting across her face. "As the both of you know, quite a few years before I ever met your father, I was held captive by a man named Marcus Humer."

"We know," Bree whispered, putting her hand over Viv's.

I tensed beneath the blankets; not sure I wanted to hear this story the night before I made my way out into the world. But then again, maybe it was the best time to hear it.

"Well, one thing I've never told you is how it happened. How before he was able to take me captive, I walked into his trap willingly." Her gaze found mine. "He was charming and handsome and knew exactly how to make me fall for him."

"Mom," I murmured. "Why are you telling us this now?"

"I don't want to scare you, sweetie. I just want you to prepare yourself for what you might find out there. Don't blindly trust anyone, and for Neros' sake, trust your instincts. When I met Humer, my stomach was in knots, but I blamed it on excitement and ignored it." She scooted closer to us, reaching over to take my hand. "Shifters have better instincts than non-shifters. Make sure to listen to them."

"I will, Mom," I promised.

"Me too!" Bree chimed in.

Viv pulled us both into a hug, holding us tightly. When she left, Bree leaned onto my shoulder and sighed. Neither of

us spoke again, both seemingly lost in our thoughts until we fell asleep.

Bree woke me in the morning.

"Can we go for one last swim together?" she asked, keeping her voice quiet.

I blinked rapidly, trying to wake myself up enough to respond.

Groaning, I rolled toward her. "Give me five minutes."

Twenty minutes later, we were diving into the lake and shifting beneath the ripples.

The water was invigorating. It cleared my mind and woke me up fully. I tried to take in the moment with my sister and let it soak into every part of me, so I'd remember it when I missed her the most.

When we returned home, Lia, Jami, Marley, Nix, and Jami's first mate Garret were waiting to leave. Apparently, Lia had decided to spend some time with Jami on his ship, so she was joining us.

"Sorry, I needed one last swim with my sister," Bree said, giving me a quick hug.

Viv had tied my bag to the saddle of the horse I'd be sharing with Nix. I was ready to go.

I tried to keep my goodbyes short, not dwelling on how much I'd miss everyone. Like Finn had said, I could come home whenever I wanted. But I wouldn't cave too soon. I promised myself I'd at least make it a few weeks out on my own before thinking about going home.

My time in Thalassia had prepared me for this.

"Time to go," Nix said, helping me up into the saddle. She climbed up behind me and took the reins. "We'll take good care of her," she called back to my parents.

The trek to the port would take us two days, so we had to stop at an inn along the way. Marley, Nix and Garrett shared a room, while Jami and Lia shared another. I had my own room. They said it was my first step into independence or something cheesy.

But I took that to heart and decided to go out that night to the bar down the road. I let Lia know before I left, and she promised to check in at some point, but didn't try to join me, which I couldn't believe. Marley and Nix, of course, were already at the bar with Garrett.

"Fancy seeing you here miss Nora," Marley teased, handing me a glass of some brown liquid. I guessed it was whiskey, which my dad preferred, but it wasn't my favorite.

Either way, I took a sip, confirming my suspicions, and put the drink down on the table they occupied before stepping away.

"I'm going to get my own drink but thank you. And, please, if you see me again, you don't know me," I said.

"Got it." Marley gave me a thumbs up. Garrett and Nix followed suit, and I rolled my eyes.

At the bar, I didn't have to wait long for a drink. I ordered a sweet wine that made me feel bubbly. The perfect drink for my first night on my own, kind of. I could pretend, anyway.

I sat on one of the bar stools and faced the room. There were some tables, all full, and a small dance floor on the opposite side of the room. Despite the crowd seeming a bit

tamer, the dance floor was full. The music was fun, upbeat, and danceable. So, when I finished off my first wine and received my second, I headed for the dance floor. I wouldn't want to meet someone on the sidelines, anyway.

Much to my disbelief, Finn used to love dancing in bars like this. And if I wanted to find a love like my parents', then I'd try out some of their tricks.

At first, it felt a little awkward dancing alone, but then it turned into a whole other sensation. *Freedom.* I laughed aloud to myself, probably making everyone around me think I was crazy, but I couldn't care less.

This entire trip was all about finding what made me happiest and living my best life. If dancing alone while drinking wine was one of those things, then I'd discovered something new about myself. I wouldn't hold back from indulging in anything that made me happy.

A prickling sensation washed over me, and I sensed I was being watched. At first, I assumed it was Marley or Nix, but when I looked at their table, they were all engaged playing some drinking game.

Turning to the bar, I scanned the people until my gaze locked with pitch black eyes, which matched the man's short, black, wavy hair. His tunic revealed his forearms which were covered in tattoos, and the triangle of skin showing on his chest revealed he had at least one there as well. His eyes only left me when he lifted his head to take a sip of his drink, and *gods ...* The way his throat bobbed when he swallowed.

I turned away, my face flushed, and other parts of me as well. Gripping my wine glass like a lifeline, I chugged the contents of it and took deep breaths, trying not to panic.

Marc had been attractive, but nowhere near as gorgeous as the man I could feel still staring at me from the bar.

Maybe just one more look ... I tried to make it seem like I was still dancing, and not trying to sneak another peek at the man, but he smirked as if he knew exactly what I was doing. On my next rotation, though, he was gone, and I deflated. It was possible I'd imagined him. That made the most sense, anyway.

Leaving the dance floor, I headed toward the bar, but a hand caught mine and I turned back.

"Looking for something?" The man from the bar was inches from me, staring down into my eyes, unwavering. "Or someone?" He bit his bottom lip, and I thought I might turn into a puddle, right then and there.

I opened my mouth to respond, but no words came out. Up close, I could see a scar next to his left eye, and another running down the length of the right side of his neck. My gaze snagged there, and he cleared his throat, releasing my hand.

"My mistake," he said, backing away.

Acting without thought, my hand shot out and grabbed his. "No. I mean, do you want to dance?"

He smiled, and I thought he was going to say yes, but he said, "No."

As disappointing as that was, he obviously wasn't the guy for me.

"Then I'm no longer interested." I shrugged and let go of his hand, prepared to scrub him from my brain, no matter how long that took.

"I'm sorry, dancing is your deal breaker?" he teased.

"Tonight it is, yes," I said matter-of-factly.

Cocking his head to the side so that a swoop of his hair moved and covered his eye, making me swoon inwardly, he asked, "What about tomorrow night?"

"Tomorrow night you'll have missed your chance and I'll be gone from your life forever," I said, closing the distance between us and smiling up at him sweetly. "Too bad." I moved to walk past him, but he caught me and twirled me into a low dip, taking my breath away, and leaving his face mere inches from mine.

"If you tell anyone about this, I'll have to kill you," he said low enough so only I'd hear. My legs turned to pudding and if he didn't have his arms around me, I'd be on the floor.

"Fair enough," I managed to say while he steered us back onto the dance floor.

I had been entirely prepared to let this man walk out of my life, but now I had no idea how to act or what to say. True, I'd still be leaving in the morning and most likely never see him again, but I was living in the moment. Pretending tomorrow didn't exist.

Our twirling and dipping tamed down and I put my arms up on his shoulders, clasping my hands behind his head and met his gaze once more. His hands moved to my waist and his thumbs traced circles on my hips, driving me crazy.

"What's your name?" I asked, realizing we'd completely skipped over that basic question. It also reminded me that I was *Sonora.* At least until the threat on my life passed.

"Oh, you think you've earned that, do you?" he asked. His right hand left my hip, and his thumb brushed along my jaw.

"I do. I got you to dance with me, so I say I've earned the right to know your name," I said. I wasn't going to let him

35

intimidate me, or try to talk circles around me, which I could guess he was entirely capable of doing.

His gaze lifted to the ceiling. "Huh. Maybe."

"If you think I'm doing anything else, just to learn your name, then you should know I'm not that kind of woman." I narrowed my eyes at him, and we stopped swaying.

He raised his eyebrows and smirked. "And you think I'm that kind of man?"

Heat crept up my neck and I dropped my hands to my sides. "I should go. I have to be up early in the morning."

"If you say so," he said, lifting his shoulder in a half shrug. "It was a pleasure meeting you, and much to my surprise, not so horrible dancing with you."

Biting my lip to hide my smile, I nodded. "It was nice to meet you as well. Whoever you are."

He chuckled as he walked away. I wasn't alone long before Marley sidled up to me and bumped her hip against mine.

"Fun first night of freedom?" she teased. She'd seen everything, I knew. But I couldn't bring myself to care.

"Yes. But now I'm ready for bed."

"Oh, yes. It is exhausting having to socialize." She looped her arm through mine and steered us toward the door. I couldn't help but glance back to try and find a familiar set of black eyes, watching me leave, but he was gone.

Adrian

As soon as the sun rose above the horizon, I mounted my horse and headed full speed back to the port.

Kerrigan had sent me to a few taverns and inns further inland to hang his wanted posters, and somehow, I'd wound up staying in a town with the most intriguing woman I'd ever met. And now I had to return to my life and forget about her.

Impossible.

There was a reason I hadn't given her my name or asked hers. I thought it would make it easier to forget her. But it wouldn't.

Rain drizzled from the sky, not enough to make me want to pull off the road and wait it out, but enough to make me uncomfortable. The discomfort distracted me from the memory of *her.* The feel of her skin beneath my fingertips and her hands twisting at the back of my neck. I could imagine them other places ... *Fuck.*

By the time night fell, I'd dropped my horse off in a stable and made it to my favorite bar in the port, The Broken

Barrel. I was determined to drink enough to erase my memories of the night before.

I *danced* with her. I shuddered. If any of the crew had found out about that, I'd never have heard the end of it. No woman had ever gotten me on the dance floor before, and I would never let it happen again.

"Adrian," Polly called and waved me over to the table she sat at with some of our other crewmates. "Welcome back, have a drink." She held a glass of rum up to me and I took it, gulping it down.

"Good to be back." I sat beside her and waved down a waitress to get me another drink. "What did I miss?"

"Only Nate being a jackass to the locals," Polly said, pointing to our crewmate across the table.

Nate shrugged. "They shouldn't be so stubborn. All I wanted was to see a show."

"That started an hour prior! You can't expect to be let in mid performance. You'd ruin the whole thing!" Polly broke into a fit of laughter. "They threw him out on his ass."

I laughed along with her. "I wish I'd been there to see it."

"It will happen again, I'm sure," Polly said. "What about you? Have any stories from your excursion?"

"Not a single one," I said, knocking my knuckles on the table.

Polly leaned in a little closer and lowered her voice as she said, "Don't go trying to pick any fights tonight. There's a new crew in town searching for the same girl Captain Kerrigan is, and he's in a foul mood."

"Duly noted." I nodded my thanks and had no intention of heeding her advice. A good fight was exactly what I needed. Especially if it would piss off Kerrigan even more that night.

But first I needed more rum. The waitress arrived just in time to deliver, and I sipped my glass a bit more slowly than the first drink I'd had, scanning the room for a good target. I didn't want it to be an easy fight, so I needed someone a little larger than myself.

Gotcha, I thought when my gaze locked on the perfect opponent. He was already swaying, which meant he was drunk enough to start the fight if I egged him on.

After I finished my drink, I set my glass down and left the table. No one questioned where I was going, they were used to me disappearing.

The man I approached was only a few inches taller than me, but he was heavier, and a bit buffer. One bite from my snake fangs would take him down, just like anyone else, but I kept my fangs retracted.

I walked past him, knocking my shoulder into his and making him drop his drink.

"Oh, wow. So sorry mate," I said, keeping my tone flat and my face blank.

He roared and slammed into me. It worked every time. I let him land his first few punches, glad to feel something other than the torment and longing due to my memories from the night before.

I shoved him away from me, sending him crashing into someone else who decided to join the fight.

The more the merrier, I thought.

The first guy came at me again, but I dodged his swing and landed one of my own to his side, knocking the wind out of him. The other guy came up behind him and slammed him to the ground. I was about to join in, but my eyes caught on the door to the bar opening and I froze.

As if my thoughts had miraculously conjured her, the woman from the night before walked in. She scanned the bar, passing over me at first, but her gaze flicked back to me, and she seemed as surprised as I was at what she saw. And then my feet were swept out from under me and I wound up flat on my back, a fist coming for my face. I rolled out of the way and winced at the crack of the fist hitting the floor instead.

Why is she here? I thought as I jumped to my feet and swung my fist at the nearest body, sending them sprawling to the ground.

Did she follow me?

No. She'd looked way too surprised to see me.

I tried to find her again, but she'd moved away from the door. Scanning the bar, I found her ordering a drink. She wore her hair unbound tonight, and her curls brushed the bottom of her shoulder blades as she swayed to the music. The men on either side of her smiled at her and I wanted to pull them off their stools and remind them not to lust for someone that wasn't theirs.

The wind was knocked out of me as someone kicked me in the side. Instead of retaliating, I walked away. Someone shouted behind me, but I ignored them. Rather than walking straight over to the bar and claiming her as I yearned to, I returned to the table and sat beside Polly.

She shook her head and gave me a once over. "I see you took my advice," she huffed. "But I've never seen you walk away from a fight like that before, so I'll pretend that it was because you finally had some sense knocked into you."

"Something like that," I muttered, dragging my finger through one of the condensation rings on the table from my refilled glass.

"That's a new face," Nate said, jerking his head at someone behind me. Without looking, I knew exactly who he was talking about, but I couldn't help myself. I turned and saw her with someone else's arms around her on the dance floor.

Nope. Not happening.

"Hands off, Nate," I said, trying to keep my tone light so he wouldn't think I cared *too* much.

"But I saw her first!" he argued.

Pushing away from the table, I strode for the dance floor. I had no intention of dancing that night, but I wouldn't sit by and watch her dance with someone else either.

When the other man spun her, she saw me coming and the smile slipped from her face. But she didn't move away from him.

I walked up right behind him and gripped his shoulder, surprising him apparently, because he whipped his head to me.

"I'm cutting in," I sneered.

Looking me up and down, he scoffed. "No, you're not."

"I wasn't asking." I let my fangs slide out and ran my tongue along them. "Go. Now."

Stumbling back, he hurried off the dance floor and disappeared into the crowd.

"Did you have to do that?" my new favorite voice asked.

Turning to face her, I couldn't hide my smile. My fangs hadn't retracted, but she didn't seem all that surprised by them or my antics.

"I should have known you were a shifter," she said. "I'm assuming you're not here to dance?" Her gaze shot past me to where I'd been fighting earlier. The other two men were still there, looking not too much worse than when we'd started our fight, but they sat nursing drinks.

"No. I'm not here to dance tonight," I said, my jaw clenching and skin heating at the thought of touching her again.

"But maybe tomorrow night?" She cocked an eyebrow and smirked.

"Afraid not, sweetheart."

"Hm. Shame." She tried to turn away, but I caught her wrist and lightly pulled her closer. Her smile tugged at my insides, making me feel things I thought I'd snuffed out years ago.

"I'll give you a pass on the dancing if you tell me one thing," she said. My gaze followed her tongue as she swiped it over her bottom lip.

"What's that?" I asked, though I had a good guess what it was.

"Your name." She batted her eyes and placed her hand on my chest. "Or else you'll never see me again."

I was about to cave when Kerrigan entered my field of vision.

"Sorry, sweetheart. Not tonight." I brushed my lips over her forehead and stepped around her to meet my father halfway so he wouldn't encounter her.

"I assume you finished the job," Kerrigan said when I approached him.

"There are wanted posters in every inn and bar from here to Rutberg." I hadn't *actually* gone that far, but he wouldn't know that. I didn't even particularly know where Rutberg was, just that it was somewhere toward the middle of the kingdom of Asmara.

Kerrigan grunted. "Good. I'm thinking of sailing down to the tip of Lanteria and spreading the word there as well. Maybe Sylvane if nothing comes of that."

Sailing. That would mean leaving *her* behind. Maybe that was for the best. We were pirates, after all. We were going to leave port eventually.

We made our way to our crew's table and Polly seemed nervous. She probably thought Kerrigan had somehow heard about my fight. He didn't often come out to bars, and whenever he did, he brought the mood down considerably.

"Morning after tomorrow, we're setting sail for Lanteria," Kerrigan announced to the table. "Get your fun in tonight and tomorrow night."

I couldn't help but scan the room, but there was no sign of *her*. Maybe she'd keep her word, and I'd never see her again.

Nora

In the morning, I ate breakfast alone. I couldn't be seen with Marley because she was much too recognizable, even all these years later, as Finn's right-hand woman. Nix sat a few tables over, because she was less recognizable, but we still didn't want to take too many risks. Being here was risky enough as it was.

I must have been especially broody though, because Nix came over and dropped into the seat beside me.

"Something's bothering you," she stated. "Do you want to talk about it?"

My first instinct was to say, '*no,*' but I thought better of it. She might have some advice on what my next move should be: forget about mystery man or give him one last chance.

"Promise me you won't tell Mom and Dad next time you check in with them," I said, knowing she may not keep the promise, but it was worth a shot.

"Fine."

I let out a long breath. "Okay. You remember the man I danced with the other night? When we stopped at that inn?"

She nodded.

"Right. So, interestingly enough, when I went to The Broken Barrel last night, he was there."

Her eyes widened slightly, but she said nothing, so I continued and pushed some leftover crumbs from my pastry around my plate, trying to distract myself from Nix's facial expressions.

"I was dancing with someone else, and he cut in. But when I tried to talk to him, to find out some basic things like his *name,* he suddenly had to be elsewhere. I didn't stick around to see what he did next, I just needed to get out of there."

I glanced up at Nix. She was biting her cheek as she considered her answer. Nerves made butterflies break out in my stomach.

Nix took my hand and held it on top of the table. "I won't lie and say he looked like the kind of man who is going to make things easy for you. He honestly looked like the kind of man who has a few dead bodies in his basement that need disposing of."

I opened my mouth to protest, but Nix put her hand up.

"Your dad gave off similar vibes when I first met him. That being said, don't let his prettiness or charm cloud your judgement. This is your first time out and about on your own, it's easy to latch onto the first person who throws a few glances your way. It took your mother hundreds of years to find the love of her life."

I deflated a little. Maybe she was right. Maybe I was only so interested in him because he was the first man I'd come across since going out on my own and he said some intriguing things. Not among those things was his name, though, which seemed kind of important.

"You're right. I should try and enjoy my freedom a bit longer before wasting my time with some guy who won't even tell me his name." I huffed a long breath. "I'll try out a different bar tonight."

"You should spend some time in the port during the day today, it's a whole different experience. The shopping is top tier, according to Marley." Nix smiled, as she always did when she spoke of Marley. It reminded me of the story of how they got together, which Marley had told me often when I was younger. It hadn't been easy for them at the start, and Nix had been quick to say that it was mostly Marley's fault for being so confusing.

Maybe I shouldn't give up hope for mystery guy just yet, I thought. I would still try out a new bar that night, but if he happened to be there, I wouldn't mind talking to him one more time. Who was I to deny fate anyway?

We were staying at The Flight Deck Inn, and it was a short walk down to the port. I figured I'd see if Marley was right about the shopping.

Even though I knew either Marley or Nix was close by while I walked from stall to stall on the pier, it was still strange to be alone among all those people. No one paid much attention to me, and it was freeing. I wasn't expected to be anywhere or do anything, and I moved at a leisurely pace. No one was waiting for me or kept me from stopping at all the stalls.

So, I did. I stopped at every single stall and storefront on the pier. Even the ones I didn't particularly care about, like a weapons store. It seemed to be mostly knives and daggers, which normally I wouldn't have much interest in, but there was one that caught my eye.

The jagged blade reminded me of Lia's dagger she carried. *It does more damage this way,* she said when I asked her why it wasn't a straight blade like most I'd seen.

The one I looked at in the glass case had pearls embedded in the hilt that looked like a seashell. It would make a good gift for Lia, to thank her for letting me stay with her in Thalassia.

The doorbells jangled as someone else walked into the store and the man behind the front counter at my back greeted them.

"Adrian, I wasn't expecting you today," he said, sounding a bit nervous.

I was tempted to turn and see why he'd be so nervous about this *Adrian,* but I didn't want to draw attention to myself if they truly were a nerve-wracking presence.

"Our plans changed, and we'll be heading out in the morning. We'll need those new weapons ready to be picked up tonight."

I sucked in a sharp breath. I recognized that voice.

Adrian. Finally, a name to put with his beautiful face.

The floor creaked right behind me and I jumped, whirling around and coming face to face with Adrian.

"Don't think I didn't recognize you, even from behind sweetheart," he said, low enough so the shopkeeper wouldn't hear. "I definitely wasn't expecting to find you *here.*"

"I wasn't expecting to find you either, *Adrian.*" I bit my lip trying to hide my amusement.

He looked at the dagger I'd been admiring and then turned back to the shopkeeper.

47

"Add this one to my father's tab. She'll be taking it," he said.

"Yes, sir." The shopkeeper sprang into action, coming over to the case in front of me and unlocking it swiftly to get me my new dagger.

I shook my head. "I don't need—"

"See you around, sweetheart," Adrian said before slipping back out the front door.

"Here you are, miss," the shopkeeper said.

I turned to face him, and he held the dagger out to me. He'd tucked it in a deep purple leather sheath with gold accents.

"Uh, thank you." I took it, unsure what else to do. He dipped his head to me and returned to the other side of the shop.

Leaving quickly, I tried to see if Adrian was still around, but there were far too many people blocking my view. It was useless.

Adrian. It seemed like fate that I'd been in that shop when he walked in. Maybe the gods *wanted* me to keep running into him. Maybe we were meant to be ... *No.* I shook my head and pinched my arm.

"You're being a love-struck idiot," I chastised myself. "Remember what Nix said." I steeled myself and headed back to the inn. I would stick to my plan and go to a different, random bar that night.

When I was safe in my room, I flopped face down onto my bed, dropping the dagger beside me.

"Find anything fun out there?" Marley asked, making me scream as I jumped off the bed and flung a pillow in her direction.

48

Knocking the pillow out of the air, Marley laughed. "You left your window open. I'm just trying to show you how easy it would be to break in if someone were trying to steal you away."

I straightened my tunic and crossed my arms over my chest. "*You're* going to be the death of me. Not some random person trying to steal me away through a window on the third floor." Marley was a hawk shifter, so probably one of few people who would be able to come in through my window so easily.

She shrugged and skipped over to my bed, picking up the dagger. "What's this?" she asked, taking it out of its sheath. "Ooh, fancy. Reminds me of Lia's."

"That's what I thought too."

"Must have cost you all the money in your purse. How did you afford this?" Her eyes narrowed and she pointed the dagger at me. "Did my lessons finally pay off?" She smirked.

"No!" I hissed. "I didn't steal it!" I tried to grab the hilt from her, but she moved it out of reach. She was a few inches taller than me. "Adrian bought it for me."

Marley cocked her head to the side. "Adrian?" She sheathed the dagger and handed it back to me. "Is that the boy you told Nix about this morning?"

"Of course she told you about him." I hadn't expected her to keep it from Marley forever, but she could have shown a *little* restraint. "Yes. It's the same person."

"So, he has a name now!" Marley teased. "How exciting."

I didn't add that I was pretty sure he was a pirate, since he'd said to the shopkeeper that they needed their weapons early because they were headed out in the morning.

She didn't need to know, and I could be wrong. Maybe they were traveling merchants and needed weapons to protect themselves.

"I'm going to take a nap now, so if you wouldn't mind," I said, waving her off my bed.

"I recognize this as a ploy to get rid of me, but I will concede. Only so that I can go investigate this *Adrian* a little more." She winked before shifting into a hawk and hopping out the window.

I groaned and sat back on my bed, praying she wouldn't find him. There was an image of her harassing him and scaring him away from me forever replaying in my mind.

After my nap, I ate dinner alone and then decided to change into one of the dresses I'd bought that day. I was normally a tight tunic and leggings kind of girl, but the dresses here were so pretty. I had to try them out.

I picked one that was flowy and stopped mid-calf, giving me plenty of freedom to move around, but it hugged my hips and upper body. It almost matched the purple of the dagger's sheath. The straps were thick and didn't dig into my skin, and there was a tie over my chest that I tightened enough to give myself a little lift. I wasn't particularly busty, but it gave me the illusion of having more than I did, which I appreciated.

Last minute, I chose to tie my dagger around my upper thigh beneath my dress, using a ribbon that had been used as a little décor for my clothes bag. It slipped a little at first, but once I tightened it, it stayed put.

I toyed with my hair for a few minutes and settled on pulling it up and letting a few pieces frame my face. It was hot in Asmara, especially this time of year, and I didn't want my hair

sticking to me. I'd inherited my dad's wavy, and sometimes a bit unruly, hair, that the heat did nothing to help. It wasn't too bad that night though. It could almost pass as styled, even though I'd never styled it before other than to braid it or wrangle it into a bun.

I hadn't thought about buying new shoes, so all I had was my leather lace-up boots. They didn't look horrible with my dress, and they'd be more convenient for walking and dancing than some of the heeled shoes I'd seen women wearing the night before.

The first bar I stopped at in the port had no dance floor, so I left after one drink. It took me a few more bars before I found one that had both a dance floor and people *dancing*. I didn't want to be the only one.

Once I started dancing though, I wasn't having much fun. There were a few other women who danced near me and sort of included me in their group, which was nice, but it didn't take long before I got bored and decided to find a table to sit down.

There was one empty high-top table at the edge of the bar near the front door and I took it. I was content watching people interact rather than trying to interact with anyone myself. I wouldn't admit it to myself, but there was only one person I cared to talk to, and he wasn't around.

I was about to get up and leave when the door opened, and a few men and women trickled in.

The first man was complaining. "I can't believe we're coming *here* for our last night in port. This isn't even the third best bar," he groaned.

The woman behind him rolled her eyes. "You're free to leave and spare us all the dramatics," she grumbled. Two others behind them sniggered as they all sidled up to the bar.

Then the door opened again, and Adrian sauntered in. He held a piece of parchment in his hand that he hung beside the door before following the others who had walked in and took the only open bar stool at the bar, putting his back to me.

I sat completely still, as if it would camouflage me if he looked my way, but he didn't.

"*No fighting* tonight," the woman told Adrian. "And I mean it. I'll drag you out of here myself."

"I don't know why you bother, Polly. It's inevitable at this point that his night will end in some kind of brawl or mass murder," the man who'd been complaining said.

Nix's words lit up like a warning sign in my mind. *He looked like the kind of man who has a few dead bodies in his basement that need disposing of.*

Oh gods. Sweat trickled down my back. I could never let her know she was right. I'd never hear the end of it.

I thought about what Viv had told me, to trust my instincts, and I studied Adrian for a few seconds trying to determine if I had any warning bells. But there was nothing. That didn't mean he wasn't a *murderer* though.

Glancing at the door, I wondered if I could sneak out without him seeing me. He seemed focused on getting a drink and his friends, or crewmates, whatever they were, blocked his line of sight to the door, so he might not see me.

Of course, the entire time I considered all that, I'd been staring a hole into the back of Adrian's head, and he must have

sensed it because he turned my way. It seemed he also had decent instincts.

I wanted to shrink down in my seat and try to hide, but instead I sat up tall and gave him what I hoped was a look that said, 'I'm not afraid of you and I'm not trying to run away right now.' Kind of a smirk and raised eyebrow that possibly made me look confused instead of my intended outcome.

His face remained impassive, and he turned back, not making any move to indicate he cared I was there. Despite my desire to run a few moments prior, disappointment filled me.

Turning to the man beside him, he said something I couldn't hear, but the response was loud and clear.

"Oh, thank the gods! Come on, let's get out of here." And then they all left. Adrian didn't even glance my way before strolling out the door.

Well, I guess that's that.

I waited a few minutes before I hopped from my chair and went to see what Adrian had hung beside the door. My blood ran cold, and panic clawed its way up my throat.

"Shit," I gasped.

Wanted
Leonora Harper
Daughter of Finnian and Vivianne Harper
Known mermaid shifter

If found, deliver ALIVE to Captain Kerrigan

Glancing around, I made sure no one was looking when I ripped the poster down and crumpled it up, shoving it into the

trash. I hurried outside and slammed full body into a wall of a man.

He grabbed my wrists and held them in place against his chest where I'd accidentally put them to stop myself. His long, black hair came forward as he leaned down and put his face closer to mine, while his large tricorn hat grazed my forehead.

Cringing, I tried to pull away, but he held me too tightly.

"You should watch where you're going, young lady," he snarled, his lip curling up into a half smile. He could have been handsome at some point in his life, but age and cruelty had stolen that, leaving a terrifying visage.

"I—I'm sorry. Please, release me," I said, trying to keep my voice even. I didn't want him to know how afraid I was.

His grip only tightened, and in a panic, my claws slid out, piercing the front of his tunic and chest, drawing blood. Except, much to my surprise, they weren't my mermaid claws, which were more like elongated nails. These were darker, and more curved. *Like a lion's claws.*

The man shoved me away and I fell to the cobblestones, scraping my knees and palms.

"I'm sorry!" I cried. "I'm a mermaid and my claws come out when I panic!" I lied, praying he wouldn't retaliate, or recognize that those had *not* been mermaid claws.

I yipped as he grabbed my hair and pulled my head back. His hot breath warmed my ear as he growled, "I will *end* you for daring to lay a hand on me."

A single tear slipped down my cheek.

Something across the street caught my eye, the glint of a weapon. A flash of red hair told me Marley was coming to my

rescue, but before she appeared, footsteps came from behind me and the man.

"Captain!" *Adrian.* A familiar voice, and one that would have been welcomed if I hadn't found out it belonged to the person trying to capture me and sell me to the highest bidder. Now I had to wonder if he knew who I was this whole time and only paid me any mind because he'd hoped to get me alone and kidnap me.

Oh my gods, my mother warned me of this exact situation, I couldn't help thinking.

The man released me and straightened.

"Adrian. Just in time. I worried I might have to dirty my own hands with this one, but you can take care of her for me."

I took the opportunity to get back on my feet and faced the two men. Adrian appeared as calm and collected as ever, which sent a bolt of anger through me.

He motioned to the man's chest, smirking. "You've got something there."

"That bitch got her claws into me. I always knew I hated mermaids." He brushed his hands over his breeches as if wiping my germs from him.

I'm cleaner than you, asshole, I thought, doing my best to keep my own disgust from showing on my face.

Adrian's gaze darted to me briefly. More people walked up behind him, and as relief flooded me, it was quickly replaced with fear as I realized they were all *with* Adrian and the other man he'd called *Captain.*

"Captain Kerrigan, what happened to you?" someone asked.

Shit, shit, shit. Captain Kerrigan had been the name of the pirate looking for me on Adrian's poster.

"I'm glad you could all make it to the show. Adrian was just about to show this poor girl what happens when someone messes with me and my crew." Captain Kerrigan turned his head to look at me over his shoulder and sneered.

"Ah." Adrian stepped around the captain. "As it happens, there won't be that kind of show tonight." He made it to my side and slipped his arm around my waist. I started to pull away, but he leaned down and pressed his mouth close to my hair, as if being affectionate. "I'm saving your life, don't do anything stupid," he whispered.

Trying again to feel for my instincts, there were no warning bells, though my heart was beating so fast I thought I might pass out. That was more from almost being killed by Captain Kerrigan.

I forced a smile and remained rigid by Adrian's side. If I called out for Marley, she'd try to save me, but there were too many people. She couldn't take them all on. And, if she was spotted, then everyone would know who I was, and I'd never be allowed to leave home again. So, instead, I decided to see where this would lead.

Captain Kerrigan turned and placed his hand on the hilt of his sword. I hadn't noticed it before.

"Explain. Before I kill her myself," he said.

Adrian's hand tightened briefly on my waist. "As it happens, I was hoping to keep this from you, at least until we returned from Lanteria, but fate has intervened. I'd like to introduce my betrothed," he paused. I knew his name, but I'd never told him mine.

"Sonora Livingston," I said, holding my hand out to Captain Kerrigan, even though I never wanted him to touch me again. He took it briefly and dropped it like it was cursed. "But everyone calls me Nora." I'd stolen the last name from one of the authors of one of my books back home.

A few of the crew whispered, clearly intrigued by the whole situation, or amused. I couldn't tell.

Captain Kerrigan raised a brow. "My, my. What a surprise. It seems congratulations are in order then."

"Thank you, father," Adrian said.

I sucked in a breath and held it. *Father?* This kept going from bad to worse with every passing second.

"I should be getting her home. I wouldn't want her making any more trouble tonight."

Captain Kerrigan shook his head. "Oh no. She should join us on our journey to Lanteria. I wouldn't want her missing her *betrothed* too much. And Adrian." He leaned closer to the two of us. "If for some reason she doesn't make it onto the ship, and slips away, because it turns out you've *lied* to me, I'll ensure Morgan disposes of you in Nora's place."

Adrian didn't miss a beat. "Perfect. If I didn't have complete faith in her love for me, I might be worried you'd scare her away, but she's not going anywhere."

"I would like to get a few things from home, if we're going to be traveling a while," I said. It wouldn't be an odd request, even if we truly were betrothed.

Turning his cold gaze on me, Captain Kerrigan said, "Of course. Morgan and Adrian will accompany you."

A woman with long, orange-tinted blonde hair stepped forward. She looked a few years younger than the captain, and

there was no kindness in her brown eyes. It must have been snuffed out a long time ago for her to be able to serve a captain such as Kerrigan. She wore a flopping hat that shadowed half of her face, making her even more menacing, if that were possible.

Morgan walked a few paces ahead of Adrian and me. Adrian had taken his arm from my waist, which I appreciated, but he held my hand, claiming Morgan was the one who needed to be convinced before his father would believe the lie of our betrothal.

We didn't say more than that in case Morgan overheard us. She didn't comment on the fact that I was staying in an inn, and I didn't provide an explanation. While she remained outside, probably to make sure I didn't try to escape out a window, Adrian came inside with me, following me all the way to my room.

He finally released my hand once we were alone, and I hissed in pain. I'd forgotten about the cuts from my fall.

"Sit," he said, motioning to the bed. I was too drained to argue. He went into the bathing chamber, and I heard the sink running. That was one of the perks of this inn, they had running water. It wasn't unusual for places to *not* have that simple amenity.

He came back with a damp towel and knelt in front of me.

I pulled back, hissing again as I put my weight on my injured hands. "What are you doing?" I asked.

He looked up at me from beneath his lashes as if the answer should be obvious. "Cleaning up the mess my father made. Your knees are bloody."

I glanced down and realized he was right. I relaxed and let him wipe the blood away.

"What now?" I asked.

"What do you mean?"

"I mean, what am I supposed to do now, just go with you to Lanteria? I hardly know you. How do I know this isn't all a trap?"

He huffed a laugh. "A trap? You think I *planned* this? I tried to stay away from you tonight. I went to a bar I would normally never be caught dead at, and somehow, there you were. So, I left. And what do you do? Run straight into the one man who would kill you on sight for daring to bump into him on the street."

I bit the inside of my cheek trying to keep from yelling at him that if he hadn't been trying to avoid me, maybe none of this would have happened.

"That doesn't answer my question," I said.

Wiping away the last of the dirt and blood on my knees, Adrian remained crouched in front of me as he said, "Selfish as it seems, yes. You have to come with me. I don't particularly feel like dying tonight."

"Your father would really kill you over this?" I asked, even though it didn't surprise me all that much. From what little I'd seen and heard from the man; he seemed the type to kill his own son to prove a point.

"I'll find a way to get you out of this, but in the meantime, pretend you like me at least." He stood and tossed the small towel onto the floor. "Gather your things. We shouldn't keep Morgan waiting."

I glanced at the window and wondered if Marley was watching in her hawk form. I should warn her what was happening, so she didn't worry about me too much.

"Can I have a few minutes alone before we go? I just ... I need a minute," I said.

"Promise you won't escape out the window?" Adrian teased, obviously not realizing how plausible that option was with Marley and Nix around.

"I promise," I said.

He nodded and stepped out of the room, closing the door behind him.

As soon as he'd gone, Marley swooped in through the opened window and shifted in front of me.

"Are you alright? No, you're hurt." She grabbed my hands and looked them over. "They'll heal. But gods," she hissed, throwing her arms around me. "Your dad is going to kill me. I should have slit Kerrigan's throat." She pulled back and sighed.

"You know Kerrigan?" I asked. It was a stupid question. Marley had been a pirate for years before she ever met Nix or chose to take on the burden of watching over me.

"Unfortunately. He took Finn's place as the most feared pirate." She grabbed my bag and moved toward the window. "Come on, we need to get out of here before they notice you're gone."

I bit my lip and didn't move.

"Nora," Marley said, a warning in her tone.

Sighing, my shoulders slumped. "I can't. I promised Adrian I wouldn't leave. If I do, his father will have him killed."

"His fath— NORA." She turned back to me fully, her eyes wide. "Adrian is Kerrigan's son? No way am I letting you go anywhere near him again!"

"You're starting to sound like my mother," I ground out. "Marley, please. Listen to me. I understand why you want to whisk me away and send me back home. But, please, I am *begging* you, let me make this choice for myself. Just this once. You can follow me and check up on me as often as you want. And if things start to look like I might be in trouble, I can just escape into the sea and shift and be back on shore in no time."

Talking about shifting reminded me of my lion claws earlier and the possible implications of that, but that was a conversation for another time. It would only convince her *not* to let me walk out that door. I would be keeping that and the *betrothal* ordeal to myself.

"I'm not ready to have a man's death on my conscience," I added.

Marley glared at me but made no move to try and force me to go with her. She would never do that.

"You're being stupid," she said. "But fine. If I were anyone else, I would drag you out that window. You're lucky Nix isn't here. She will probably kill me for letting you do this."

I ran forward and hugged her. "Thank you! Thank you! Thank you! I have my dagger," I said, lifting my skirt to show her the purple sheath on my thigh.

She only shook her head.

Pushing her toward the window, I said, "Now go. Adrian's going to wonder what's taking me so long."

"I'm going to be killed for this one ..." Marley muttered as she moved toward the window and shifted again.

I grabbed my bag and went to the door, taking a deep breath before opening it.

Adrian leaned against the opposite wall in the hall, one foot kicked back and a disinterested look on his face.

"Ready, sweetheart?" he asked.

"You owe me," I said, walking past him.

He caught up to me and took my bag. "It would be remiss for me to allow my betrothed to carry her own bag," he explained. He was having too much fun with this whole thing. "And I think it's *you* who owes *me*. I saved your life out there."

"I can take care of myself," I snapped.

"Mm. Sure. We'll see about that."

He held the front door open for me. Morgan met us as soon as we stepped outside and led the way again.

There were far fewer people on the pier now, and none of them looked our way. They were all much too drunk to see anything beyond their own two feet.

The gangplank leading up to the ship creaked underfoot when I stepped onto it, and I hesitated. I'd been on Jami's ship before, but this wasn't Jami's ship. I had no idea what to expect aboard this vessel, and who I might encounter.

Adrian rested his hand on the small of my back.

"I've got you," he murmured. I didn't know if he meant that he wouldn't let me fall, or if he meant he wouldn't let any harm come to me, but I chose to believe the latter.

There were only a few crew members on the deck when we arrived. I assumed everyone else was either sleeping or still at the bars.

62

"Show her to your room and then Captain Kerrigan wants to see you in his quarters," Morgan said to Adrian. She didn't even glance at me before stalking away.

"This way," Adrian said, steering me toward a set of stairs to the left of what looked to be the captain's quarters. "Luckily for you, we have our own room."

"*We?*" I hadn't thought about the possibility of having to share a room with him. I got hot and cold all at once.

"Don't worry, sweetheart, I don't bite," he teased, baring his elongated snake fangs.

"Keep those things away from me," I warned, surprised at the shiver of excitement that ran through me.

"Only because you asked so nicely." He retracted them.

The stairs creaked as we reached the lower level, and Adrian opened the door directly in front of us. It was the smallest bedroom I'd ever seen, and half the space was taken up by the door when it opened. A bed barely large enough for two people and a wash bucket in the corner were the only furnishings.

"Well," I huffed.

"It's either this or a hammock surrounded by thirty other people."

I stepped into the room and sat on the bed, because there was nothing else to do. Adrian tossed my bag to the floor beside the wash bucket.

"I have to go talk with my father. There's a key in the lock." He pulled the door shut enough to show me the key sticking out of the lock on the inside of the door. "Keep this door shut and locked at all times when I'm not with you. Don't open it for anyone but me."

63

Feigning a long sigh, I said, "Ugh, I changed my mind. You're too bossy, I want a new betrothed."

"I'm serious, Nora."

It was the first time he'd used my name, and it did weird things to my insides.

"Right. Keep the door locked. Got it." I jerked my head in a nod.

As soon as he was gone, I locked the door.

Adrian

My father wasn't a patient man by any means, but I always enjoyed knowing when he was waiting on me. I did a turn around the bunks accepting some lewd remarks and congratulations from several crew members who were still awake. Only a few of them were sincere, I was under no illusion that any of them cared about me or my happiness in any way.

Once I made it to the main deck, I stopped to chat with Polly as she boarded the ship.

"I heard the news," she said. "Where'd you find the poor girl? She had to have been in a much worse situation prior to having agreed to latch herself to you."

"That's the kindest and most sincere thing I've heard all night," I said. She made a good point. If Nora knew me at all she'd have run and left me to my fate already. I wouldn't blame her.

There'd been no other clear path out of the mess she'd gotten into though and I had to imagine being stuck with me for a week or two was better than being dead. Maybe.

"If you don't mind keeping an eye on her when I'm not around, you're the only person on this ship I halfway trust." I hated to ask it of anyone, but Polly would do it and she wouldn't complain.

"Aye. I'll do my best but no promises," she said.

"That's all I can ask."

"Adrian!" Kerrigan yelled from the door of his quarters.

I grinned at Polly who shook her head. "Whoops! I tested his patience a bit too long. Best be going." Slipping away from her, I turned on my heel and headed for Kerrigan.

Polly harrumphed and disappeared down the stairs.

Kerrigan's eyes blazed with fury. "When I tell you to come to my office, that does not mean make ten pit stops on the way and waste my time!"

I practically danced past him in my glee to see him so angry and said, "Technically Morgan told me—"

CRACK.

The back of his hand snapped across the space between us and jerked my head to the side. That would leave a mark.

Rubbing my jaw, I ground it to keep from spitting venom at him. My fangs had protracted from the impact, and I'd bit my tongue. Thankfully I couldn't be affected by my own venom.

I spit blood onto the floor.

"Sit." Kerrigan commanded, taking his own seat behind his desk. "How long has this been going on? You and that woman."

Sliding the chair so it was angled slightly away from my father with my boot, I sank into it. "I've been seeing her on and off every time we come to port for two years," I lied. Two years

seemed like a good amount of time to get to know someone who was only around a few days or weeks at a time.

"Nora," he said, as if testing out her name. I wanted to rip his tongue out for it. But I remained seated with my arms relaxed at my sides. "She's a pretty girl despite her genetics."

He meant her being a mermaid, which I hadn't known about until that night.

"And there's something so familiar about her, but I can't quite put my finger on it." He mused to himself for a few seconds. "Anyway, if you ever pull a stunt like tonight again, I will let Morgan tear you apart, piece by agonizing piece, as I know she's longed to do for so long now."

I fisted my hands against my thighs and smiled. Morgan had never said as much to me, but I knew he exaggerated her hatred. He wanted to ensure a wedge remained between us, so we'd never decide to work together against him. And it worked. The seed of doubt had been planted and I'd never fully trusted Morgan or anyone else on the crew for that matter.

"Return to your plaything. I know you'll tire of her once you realize this charade has no effect on me. Just as all your other tantrums have never affected me." Kerrigan waved his hand, dismissing me.

I didn't deign to respond. Outside of his office, a few crew were headed down the gangplank back to the bars. We wouldn't be leaving port until morning, and after my chat with my father, I needed a stiff drink.

Trusting Polly to keep an eye out for Nora, I headed straight for The Broken Barrel and lost myself in a bottle of rum. The first guy to look at me the wrong way got a sloppy

punch thrown in their direction and then he laid me out on the floor with one strike. I didn't bother getting back up.

Nate and another crew member, John, dragged my ass back to the ship and left me to sleep off my drink on the hard floor of the crew's quarters.

"I guess that's one way to celebrate your betrothal," John said.

Their footsteps receded. "We should have left his sorry ass back at the bar. Let the captain deal with him for once," Nate said. They both laughed and then hammocks creaked against the beams. I assumed they'd climbed into their prospective beds.

Nate talked a big talk when it came to his annoyance of me, but I knew he'd never leave me behind or else Polly would never let him hear the end of it. That and for some reason he'd never quite been scared off by my antics like most of the rest of the crew.

Someone kicked me awake in the morning. Whoever it was, they were gone when I opened my eyes. The ship rocked and I knew I'd missed our shoving off from port.

Groaning from the stabbing pain in my head and the aches in my muscles from sleeping on the floor, I got to my feet and swayed with the ship.

"I'm surprised to see you out here rather than balls deep in that fine specimen in there." My least favorite crew member, Gregor, lurked beside his hammock.

"You talk about her ever again and I'll cut out your tongue. Maybe your eyeballs with it," I grumbled. Even though it came out halfhearted, he knew I didn't make empty threats.

But he had reminded me of the reason I was out there on the floor instead of in my bed.

I finally found my sea legs once I reached my door and knocked three times.

"Time to get up, sweetheart," I called to Nora.

There was slight movement behind the door before it cracked open and she stood there, staring at me, with a fire in her storm-gray eyes. She wore tight-fitting leggings and a brown, leather, corseted top that left little to the imagination. I'd be sure she put on more clothes before letting any of the other crew see her.

"You didn't come back last night," she said.

Putting my arm up against the doorway, I leaned in. "Did you miss me?"

"Not even a little." She took a step back, letting the door open the rest of the way. "You look horrible, by the way, and you reek of alcohol."

I hadn't thought to freshen up before coming to her. Not that I cared whether she was attracted to me. This whole betrothal was simply a means to keep her alive, and then I'd send her on her merry way as soon as possible. As soon as I figured out a way that she could leave without my father killing me.

"Perks of being a pirate, I guess." I stayed in the doorway while she grabbed something from the bed and attached it to the belt she wore. I recognized the purple color. "Nice dagger," I commented.

"Some asshole thought he could impress me by buying it for me," she quipped with a smug smirk, making me laugh.

"Fair enough. Now." I reached over her to her bag of clothes and grabbed a tunic. "Put this on over that." I eyed her corset.

She looked down at herself and frowned. "Why?" Realization dawned on her face, and she smirked, flipping her braid over her shoulder. "Am I making you uncomfortable?"

"You do realize that you're surrounded by a bunch of horny pirates who would love nothing more than to bend you over a rail and—"

"And what? Have you imagined this yourself?" she asked, stepping closer and placing her hand on my chest.

My entire body heated from the contact, and I had to bite my inner cheek to stop myself from throwing her back on the bed and showing her *exactly* what I imagined doing to her.

"Put. This. On. Please," I ground out, shaking the tunic.

She lifted a brow but took it and slipped it over her head. "Happy?"

It did nothing to quell the storm inside me, but at least no one else would see her in that corset.

"Immensely." I backed out of the room.

"I need to go to the bathroom," she said, following me. "I know it's going to be a horrible, traumatic experience, but unfortunately it's unavoidable."

"I won't make you use the head," I said. "My father has his own, private, toilet you can use."

The relief was clear on her face, and that made me *happy* for some reason. I wasn't used to caring about anyone else, and I wasn't sure I wanted it to continue. To take down my father, I couldn't have any weaknesses. Caring about Nora would give me the worst kind of weakness.

"Thank Neros," she murmured. "Or, you know, whatever god you pray to."

"I don't pray to any gods," I said. Even if I did, no god would listen to me after all the men I'd killed. I didn't think gods looked very kindly upon murderers or thieves.

"You sound like my dad," she commented. "He's never believed in the gods, but my mom on the other hand ..." She stopped abruptly.

We'd come to my father's quarters, so I didn't press her on what she'd been about to say. I knocked on the door, and when no one answered, I opened it and let Nora inside.

Pointing to a door on the left-hand side, I said, "That door there leads to his washroom. You can use the bath as well when he's not around."

"Can she?" Morgan spoke from the corner of the office. There was a wall behind my father's desk that separated his bedroom from the office.

"Go on," I said to Nora, giving her a little push toward the washroom. She hesitated, but hurried in. "I'm not going to make my betrothed use the head with the rest of the crew. Captain Kerrigan will understand my need to keep my future wife away from prying eyes in such a state of undress."

Morgan took a few steps out of the corner, leaning against my father's desk. "You're really trying to push your luck."

"I call it chivalry," I said, lifting a shoulder and smirking.

Nora came back out, glancing nervously between me and Morgan.

"Give me a moment to clean up, sweetheart. Morgan will keep you company." I entered the washroom, stripping out of

my day-old clothes and testing the already filled tub. It was warm, which meant that it was fresh and waiting for my father.

"Just how I like it," I said to myself.

"How long have you been Captain Kerrigan's first mate?" Nora asked Morgan. The walls were just as thin in my father's quarters as they were in mine.

"Twenty years," Morgan answered. I was surprised she didn't just ignore Nora.

I grabbed a cloth from the stool next to the bath and began scrubbing.

"How long have you known Adrian?" Morgan asked.

I froze. Nora and I hadn't discussed the details of our lie yet, and I'd already told my father we'd been together two years. This simple exchange could ruin our entire story.

I dunked my head under the water and jumped out of the tub, grabbing a towel and drying off as quickly as I could before wrapping it around my waist.

"Oh, wow," Nora started. "It's been at least, let me think …" She was stalling. *Good girl.*

I strolled out of the washroom, stretching my arms as if I hadn't a care in the world.

Nora's gaze raked over me before she continued, "What's it been since we met, two, three …"

"About two years, I'd say," I finished for her.

"You're a dead man," Morgan said, shaking her head.

"Oh, right." I returned to the washroom. "Better not leave my things for dear old dad to find lying around." I pulled the plug on the tub; it had a pipe that would run the water out to the ocean, and I grabbed my clothes. I had another set of clothes in my room, and I rotated them out, like most of us did.

Some of the crew didn't care about being filthy and wore the same clothes every day. They bathed in them when they got the chance, or didn't wash them at all, even though we had a crew member who washed the dirty clothes for us once a week when we were out to sea.

"Morgan, would you be so kind as to give Nora a tour of the ship while I run these down to my quarters?" I asked.

"I don't work for you," she said, but that didn't stop her from leading Nora out the door onto the main deck and doing as I asked. I was quite shocked that she did it, honestly.

In the meantime, I ran down to my room to change.

Nora

The sight of Adrian in just a towel was burned into my brain. Not only was he immaculate, but the sight of all his tattoos and scars made me want to explore his entire body and learn about each and every part of him.

I welcomed the breeze coming off the sea as Morgan and I walked around the ship, cooling me down.

"Is this your first time on a ship like this?" Morgan asked, her tone flat and bored.

I considered lying, but it wasn't unusual for mermaids to befriend pirates, so I said, "No."

"Then that makes this easier. Our ship is like any other ship you've been on. The crow's nest is up there." She pointed to it. "You know where the crew's quarters are, and the captain's quarters, and that's all you truly need to know. The galley is down that set of stairs." She waved her hand to the stairs behind us, on the opposite end of the ship as the captain's quarters.

"Okay, well, thank you," I said, not sure what else to say to her brief tour.

Turning on her heel, she moved to stand in front of me.

"You may be betrothed to Adrian, but you know nothing of the things he has endured on this ship at Captain Kerrigan's hand and behest. If you care about him, at all, you'll refuse any *special treatment*." Her lips curled with those words. "Stay out of Captain Kerrigan's quarters, and out of his way."

"I didn't ask—"

"Don't be stupid," she spat. "We're done here."

Not knowing how to act, or what to do, I stayed rooted to that spot, staring at the rail beside me, trying not to cry. I wouldn't cry, not in front of this crew, and not because of that woman.

"Where'd Morgan go?" Adrian asked as he came up beside me. He was fully clothed, obviously, though I couldn't help being a little disappointed. I must have looked upset or, maybe my eyes were still watering, because next he asked, "Are you alright?"

Rolling my shoulders back and lifting my chin, I said, "Fine. Just hungry."

He took my hand, surprising me. "Me too. Come on."

The galley was empty since everyone else had probably eaten hours ago, but there were some apples left in a bowl on a barrel.

Adrian grabbed one for himself and tossed another to me. "I'll make sure we get here in time for breakfast tomorrow."

"You mean you won't get drunk, and wind up passed out on the floor again tonight?" I asked, taking a bite from my apple. It was sweet and some of the juice dribbled down my chin. Adrian reached out and brushed his knuckle along my skin, wiping away the juice and then licked it from his finger.

The entire moment left me stunned and highly aroused.

"I'm very capable of doing both: getting drunk and passing out on the floor, and then also waking up early enough to make it to breakfast. I've had many years of practice." He went on with our conversation as if nothing had happened.

"Right." I coughed as I choked on my own spit.

"You alright?" he asked, a glimmer of amusement in his eyes.

I nodded, even though I was fighting to catch my breath, and still half stunned from before.

"Then we should talk about our betrothal, and the details surrounding it," he said. "While we have a moment alone."

"What is there to talk about?" I assumed we'd be fine just pretending to like each other, and maybe telling a few little anecdotes here and there if anyone asked questions.

"We need our stories to match," he explained. "I told my father that we've been together, on and off, for two years. That we'd see each other every time I came into port. Which means, you must live somewhere close enough that that's plausible, but obviously not *in* Asmara, since Morgan already knows you were staying at The Flight Deck Inn."

"Fine. I was staying at the inn because my parents—"

"Your parents are dead," he offered. "Polly made a good point that you wouldn't be with me unless you'd had a horrible life before. So, your parents died a few years back and you've been staying with friends or in the inn ever since and working in the brothel."

Indignation swirled up and I scoffed, "I wasn't working in a brothel! And you *won't* be telling anyone that."

Adrian laughed. "It's not real, what does it matter? Like I said, the crew knows no one would ever be with me if their life was at all decent before meeting me."

Huffing, I tried to calm myself down. "Look, I have nothing against women who work in brothels, but I am not going to pretend that I did! Everyone will know we're lying. Someone would ask me one question about working there and realize I have absolutely no idea what I'm talking about."

Adrian's head tilted as if he'd figured something out. "Nora, have you never been with a man?"

He said it much less crudely than I imagined most pirates would, which surprised me. He was doing that a lot.

"Of course I've been with a man!" I said a bit too loudly. Lowering my voice, I continued, "But that doesn't mean I'm experienced enough to pretend to have worked in a brothel."

"*A* man, singular?" he pressed.

"Why is this the most important thing right now?" I tugged on my braid and pinned my gaze to the floor.

"I feel as your future husband, I should know what I'm getting myself into," he said, moving closer and tipping my chin up with the same knuckle he'd touched me with before, so my gaze met his.

"But it's not real," I said, my voice coming out much softer than usual. He brushed his lips over mine, and as much as I wanted to press myself against him, I held myself back.

His mouth moved close to my ear, and he murmured, "No, it's not real." And then he walked away, leaving me alone in the galley.

77

A woman named Polly kept me company the rest of the day. She was very chatty, which meant I didn't need to do much talking. There was a story to go with almost all the crew members, which helped me to remember some of their names.

Nate was her closest ally. She didn't believe in friends on a pirate ship, because everyone cared about one thing above all else: gold. Duly noted. Then there was John, who she said was too nice for his own good, but not to mess with him while he was eating because he'd bite your finger off.

One-eyed Wally had one eye, obviously, how he lost it Polly didn't say, but she'd cast her gaze at Adrian. She warned me to steer clear of Gregor and Lyle. From their leering gazes, I could tell she wasn't being overly cautious.

Polly even showed me where the head was and kept everyone else away while I used it for the first time. I was right, and it was a bit of an embarrassing moment, but I knew I'd get used to it. I wasn't about to use Captain Kerrigan's washroom after what Morgan had said.

When the sun set, Polly walked me to the galley for dinner.

"Adrian has lived a hard life, so cut him some slack on his manners," Polly said. She'd pulled her long, graying blonde hair up and piled it atop her head. It made her look younger and made me realize how *pretty* she was. I didn't know why I hadn't noticed it sooner, but her eyes were bluer than the bright waters surrounding Asmara. She hunched a little, but she was still as tall as me.

"I didn't think pirates minded their manners no matter their lot," I commented, hoping I wasn't offending her.

"They don't. But Adrian's a little ... Overboard sometimes. If you haven't seen it yet, you will. Especially once we dock in Lanteria. The people there are a lot less receptive of pirates, and it's his favorite place to pick fights."

I thought of the fight he'd been in that night at The Broken Barrel, and the scars all over his body.

We joined a line at the bottom of the stairs. There was some kind of nausea-inducing slop being served, but I was so hungry I didn't complain. Polly and I found a seat beside the stairs, on two smaller barrels because all the tables were taken. Adrian found us there with his own bowl of food.

"I've got a game of cards calling my name," Polly said, leaving her seat to Adrian.

"How was your first day on a pirate ship?" Adrian asked, lifting one foot to prop it against the barrel and balanced his bowl on his knee.

"It wasn't my first day on a pirate ship," I said, setting my empty bowl aside.

His posture straightened and he asked, "Oh really? Do tell about that experience. Was it your other lover? Should I be worried about a pirate with a vengeance coming after me for stealing his mate?"

I rolled my eyes. "You are impossible to have a simple conversation with."

"That answers none of my questions." He took a bite of his slop and wrinkled his nose. "As horrible as ever," he said, but continued to eat.

"No. If you must know, my other *lover,* as you put it, was not a pirate. He was a mer shifter, like me. And you have no need to worry about him coming after you, because he broke

79

things off with me, though I was about to break things off with him—"

"Don't worry, you don't need to pretend you weren't heartbroken on my account." He held his fist in front of his mouth as he spoke with his mouth full.

My fingers curled around the hem of my tunic. "I wasn't heartbroken. It wasn't love. We both knew that. But enough about me, please tell me about the copious amounts of women you've been with, I'm dying to know." The sarcasm in my voice was evident.

Tipping the last of the contents of his bowl into his mouth, he swallowed, his throat bobbing and entrancing me for all of two seconds, before he spoke again.

"Oh, I've left a string of broken hearts in my wake. Enough to crew a whole pirate ship, I'm sure," he said, running a hand down his thigh.

I needed to change the subject, or else I might be tempted to do something stupid.

"Polly told me that Lanteria is your favorite place to pick fights," I said.

Adrian tilted his head to the side. "Oh yeah?"

"Why is that?"

He shrugged and stood. "I wouldn't say it's my *favorite*. I'll pick a fight anywhere if I want."

"Seems arrogant in my opinion." I scrunched my nose.

"It's a good thing I didn't ask for your opinion." He turned on his heel and strode to the barrel of dishes, putting his bowl on the top of the pile.

Annoyance and anger swelled inside me, and I hopped up from my seat, hurrying to the stairs. Adrian wasn't far behind.

The card game Polly had mentioned was taking place at a table to the right on the main deck, and there was an empty seat beside her.

Swerving toward the table, I took the seat. "Can I join?" I asked.

Polly nodded enthusiastically. "Next round, you're in," she said.

Nate sat across from me, and Gregor sat at the end of the table, thankfully not leering at me as he usually did.

"Get up, sweetheart," Adrian drawled, standing behind me. I refused to look at him, but he took my arm, and I snapped my head back to glare at him.

"Am I not allowed to play?" I asked, putting on a fake, sweet smile.

He raised a brow and smirked. "You didn't think I'd let you play alone, did you?"

I let him pull me out of the seat, which he sat in, and then he guided me onto his lap. No one else seemed phased by the interaction, continuing their own chatter on the side, but my cheeks were burning.

"Have you ever played before, sweetheart?" he asked, waving a hand toward the cards.

Each person held two cards in their hand and there was a discard pile and a draw pile in the center. I wasn't sure about the exact game they played, but it looked like they were trying to either make a pair or find a certain card.

"No, but I think I can figure it out," I said a bit too harshly. We were supposed to be convincing everyone that we were in love, but I was too mad at Adrian to pretend. Sitting on his lap wasn't helping anything either. His warm, muscular thighs

supporting me ... It was making me feel hot and achy in all the places I did *not* want to be feeling that in front of strangers.

Adrian rested one arm on the table, partially caging me in. "Whoever gets either a pair of royals, or the two unmarked cards first wins," he explained.

"Unmarked?" I turned my head slightly, so I could see his face.

"There are always two cards in every deck that are unmarked. All they have on them is a design matching that of the back of the cards." He jerked his head toward Polly's hand which we could see. She held one of the unmarked cards. "If someone has an unmarked card, but doesn't think they'll get the other, they can discard it like any other card, but then there's a chance the next player will have it."

I nodded in understanding.

"We use two to three decks for our games, depending on how many players there are."

Polly drew a card and let out a whoop, throwing down two unmarked cards. "Take that," she said, pulling in a pile of trinkets toward herself. "I'll be taking these."

"Winnings?" I presumed.

"Coins are precious on board a pirate ship, so we trade other things of value. They may not hold value to everyone, but they do for someone," Polly explained, winking as she slipped something from the pile into her pocket.

She shuffled the cards and dealt them onto the table in front of each person. When she came to me, I shook my head.

"I don't have anything to give away," I said.

Adrian's chest rumbled against my back as he laughed. "Don't worry, sweetheart, I'll cover the both of us." He dropped

a pocket watch onto the table. "Swiped that while we were in port."

Everyone else followed suit, throwing in things like pipes, small pieces of jewelry, compasses, and other trinkets.

Adrian had both arms resting on the table while he held our cards, and I was feeling *incredibly* warm.

I cleared my throat and readjusted on his lap, trying not to look too awkward. He let out a low hiss.

"Watch yourself, sweetheart," he murmured against my ear, twisting up my insides.

Understanding dawned on me and I bit my lip. Slowly, I leaned forward, as if looking at our cards better, and pressed my ass back a little more, feeling his cock hardening against me.

"Hm." He took our turn, drawing a numbered card and discarding it in the same movement, and then placed our cards face down on the table. One of his hands dropped down to my knee, inching slowly up my thigh and making me practically buzz from the anticipation.

Everyone around us was too focused on the game to notice what was happening under the table. My toes curled in my boots, and I leaned back against Adrian's chest.

The game was moving so quickly, it was already our turn again and Adrian's hand left my thigh, much to my dismay. He drew a royal card and discarded something ... It was too hard to focus when I was trying so hard not to give away the ecstasy I was feeling from Adrian's hard length pressing into my backside. Every small movement made me long for more.

Fuck. I was in trouble.

"Do you want to give it a try?" Adrian asked.

At first, I had no idea what he was talking about, and I stiffened, thinking his mind was in the same place as mine was. But then he held the cards toward me. He meant *the game.*

"Um, yeah." I took the cards from him and looked at them for real for the first time. *A queen and a nine.* It was our turn, so I drew a card, the movement making Adrian's cock twitch against my ass. I bit my lip. His hands were resting on my hips, and his thumbs were tracing circles against my skin beneath my tunic.

Focus. I chided myself. I'd drawn a two. I threw that down onto the discard pile. Someone to our left ended up winning that round, and the game restarted, but I was so far gone from the game. I needed to cool down.

"I think I'm going to call it a night," I said, glancing back at Adrian. "I didn't realize how tired I was."

His lips twitched as if he were fighting a smile. He knew I was lying.

"Sure, sweetheart." He scooted our chair back so I could stand, and I moved toward the stairs.

I wasn't paying much attention to my surroundings, and someone grabbed my wrist, pulling me into their lap.

"My turn, little lamb," Gregor sneered, his breath hot against my face as I tried to regain my sense of balance and break away.

A hand gripped my other arm, yanking me out of Gregor's lap. I yelped in pain, but Adrian kept his grip, holding me at his side as he glared down at Gregor. Everyone else around the table fell silent.

"Did you forget the warning I gave you this morning?" Adrian asked, deadly calm, though his grip on me said otherwise.

Gregor sucked in a breath through his teeth, whistling.

"You only said I couldn't talk about her." He tapped the side of his head as if thinking. "Nothing about *touching* her or taking a *taste.*"

I wanted to vomit. Right there, across the table filled with cards and pints of rum.

Adrian released my arm to pull my dagger from the sheath on my belt and casually leaned over Gregor, placing his hand on the back of his chair to steady himself, and held the blade right beneath his eye.

"Consider this my final warning then."

I couldn't watch this happen, no matter how vile Gregor was.

"Stop!" I put my hand on Adrian's arm, trying to pull him back.

There were a few snickers around the table.

"Adrian, I'm fine. You don't need to do this," I said.

The look of pure rage in his eyes when he turned to look at me made me take a step back, lowering my hand to my side.

"Oh, don't stop on my account," Captain Kerrigan drawled as he strolled over to the table, his hands clasped casually behind his back.

Adrian straightened, leaving Gregor with a tiny nick from the blade on his cheek.

"Sorry, Captain," Gregor muttered.

"Oh no! By all means, continue harassing the girl. I'd love to see who can push Adrian over the edge first." Captain Kerrigan shot me a sly grin. "But before this can continue, I have a score to settle with Adrian."

"Polly, take Nora to my room," Adrian said. He wiped the small amount of blood from my dagger on his pants and handed it back to me.

"No," I protested, shaking my head. "I'll stay."

Polly had already started toward me, but she hesitated.

"Polly, now." Adrian doubled down and she moved again, taking my arm and leading me away. I tried to stay where I was at first, but I didn't want to hurt Polly. She'd been the only one who'd shown me any kindness since getting on the ship.

Morgan emerged from the shadows like a ghost, stalking toward Captain Kerrigan and Adrian, while everyone else stayed seated at the card table.

"Please, Polly, let me stay," I begged, but she didn't listen, or hear over the loud chatter behind us. People were getting excited, and it made me nervous.

Once I was in Adrian's room, I turned to Polly and asked, "What's happening up there?"

She gave me a look filled with pity and then shut the door. At first, I thought I'd be able to leave as soon as she walked away, but when I tried to open the door, it had been locked from the outside.

Turning the key in the lock did nothing, because there must have been a separate locking mechanism on the other side of the door. I started banging on the door instead.

I put my ear to the door and listened as people who had been resting in their hammocks moved up the stairs. Their

words all blended together, and I couldn't make out any one conversation.

Fear and anger welled up inside me, and that tingling sensation that came with the need to shift came over me. I let out a frustrated scream, and with it, a small roar escaped my lips, and I realized my view of the world had changed.

Looking down, I had two large paws, like Finn's when he shifted into his lion form. And behind me, a tail. Panic overwhelmed me and I shifted back without trying, flopping flat onto the bed. My mother's corset that I wore had been magicked so it was still intact, but my leggings and tunic were done for.

Cries and shouts from the crew came from above me and the sound of something whistling through the air. I'd never seen anyone be whipped before, but the grunts of pain that followed each whoosh of wind told me that was exactly what was happening. The sound faded, and I realized I'd only been able to hear it with the lingering extra-sensory benefit of my lioness form.

I hid my torn clothes in my bag and pulled on a new pair of leggings before settling back on the bed. Hugging my knees to my chest, I squeezed my eyes shut. This was a nightmare. I'd been so worried about myself; I hadn't stopped to think about what I would be doing to Adrian with my actions. This was what Morgan had warned me about.

The corset I wore felt like it was suffocating me, so I reached around to untie the laces. I borrowed it from my mom's closet, and I wondered if she was missing it. Tears welled in my eyes thinking of home.

87

Once the corset was on the floor, I pulled an intact tunic from my bag and put it on. Laying on my side, I noticed my arm was sore from where Adrian had grabbed me. I hadn't been in my shifted form for long enough to heal that, but it was a stark reminder of his absence and what he was enduring.

Eventually, the commotion above me died down and I assumed Adrian would come to let me out of the room, but hours passed, and he never showed up.

Adrian

I spent the night on the floor of the crew's quarters again. Nate had lent me a tunic, since my other one had been shredded by Morgan's whip. I didn't blame her or hate her for what she'd done. It was simply orders. I'd done the same to countless other crew members over the years in place of her.

Polly tended my wounds as best she could, but I'd sent her to bed and finished wrapping them myself.

A foot nudging my ribs woke me and I grabbed it so the culprit wouldn't get away this time.

"Get off, mate," Nate hissed. "Your girl has been yelling to get out of her room for an hour now. I figured I'd save us all the grief and unlock her door, but I didn't want to meet the wrong end of your dagger."

Nora. Polly must have locked her in from the outside when she'd brought her down there last night.

I forced myself up even though my back screamed in protest. It wasn't the worst shape I'd ever been in.

As soon as I unlocked the door, Nora was there opening it from inside and throwing it against the wall, fury burning in

89

her gaze. When her eyes met mine, the anger faded, and she let out a soft breath.

"Don't *ever* lock me in here again," she said, pushing past me out of the room.

"Where are you going?" I asked, turning to her as she headed up the stairs.

She gave me an incredulous look. "I've been locked in that room since last night. I'm going to pee. Is that alright with you?"

Covering my mouth to stifle a laugh, I said, "Go ahead."

She was obviously upset with me, even though I wasn't the one who had locked her in the room. I followed her to ensure no one decided to take my father up on his game and tried to harass her. For the most part, everyone kept their distance. A few of the crew greeted her as she passed by, which surprised me. The only one who ever said good morning to me was Polly.

After she used the head, which she did without complaint, we went to the galley. There were some biscuits and salted beef left alongside the apples. The apples were usually what we ran out of first, but we had enough to last until we reached our destination this time.

Nora didn't speak to me while we ate, and she avoided looking at me. It was then that I realized she hadn't worn the tunic over her corset today. I'd been so consumed with my own pain and thoughts I'd overlooked her state of dress. She wore her hair unbound as well, which I yearned to run my hands through.

Stop. I couldn't have those thoughts right then.

"You're going back to our room and changing when we're done here," I said, rubbing my hands together to wipe the crumbs from them.

Nora's jaw moved back and forth as her eyes narrowed and I knew she was holding something back. "*Our* room," she scoffed.

"Do you have something you need to say?" I asked. The last few people who had remained in the galley when we arrived had left, and we were alone.

"I'm not changing, and I'm not going back to *our* room. Which is an odd way to label it, since you haven't been in it since I arrived."

"I've had other things going on," I defended myself. It wasn't like I'd been purposefully avoiding her. Well, maybe I had.

"I know that." Her hands twisted in her lap. "I guess I imagined this all going a little differently, is all. I don't know what I expected." She stood and I didn't follow her.

There was a lot I *should* have said. But I didn't need her thinking that I was a different man. I was a pirate through and through. A murderer, a thief, and untrustworthy. There was a reason I'd tried to avoid her the night before we left Asmara.

I made myself busy cleaning up some of the dishes and other trash. Heavy footsteps warned me someone was coming down the stairs.

"You should put a leash on that woman," Gregor commented. "Doesn't seem much like she's ready to be tied down."

I gave Gregor my best death glare. "What the fuck are you talking about now?"

He jerked his head to the stairs and then grabbed an apple. "See for yourself."

As much as I wanted to ignore him, my curiosity got the better of me.

Her laughter reached me before she came into view. I'd never heard her laugh like *that*. Granted, there were a lot of things I'd never seen or heard her do. I hadn't spent much time with her outside of the two nights we interacted briefly before getting on the ship, and I'd hardly seen her since.

She sat on the stairs leading to the upper deck and the helm, while Nate stood in front of her, foot on the stair below her while he told her some stupid story, I guessed.

What stoked the fire in me was her hand resting on his knee and the way she stared up at him as if he were the only person on the ship. She'd never given me her undivided attention like that.

Wait ... I shook my head. *Is this* jealousy?

No. This was rage. Nate didn't know that she wasn't truly mine, and he had no right to make her laugh like that.

I'd crossed the deck without realizing it and knocked Nate's leg down from the step.

"What the fuck, man?" he groused. "We were just talking. I was trying to keep Gregor and Lyle at bay."

Nora's smile disappeared, and she glared at me.

Good. Hate me.

That was when I noticed the bruises on her upper arm and nausea punched me in the gut.

"Right. Sorry," I mumbled, backing away.

I'd caused those bruises when I'd pulled her from Gregor's lap. I hadn't realized how rough I'd been with her.

Maybe Nate deserved her more than I did. He wasn't the one getting into fights every night and finding joy in killing or maiming anyone who crossed him.

The surprise on Nate's face said enough. He'd expected me to react much more violently. I wavered between giving him what he expected and walking away; between keeping up my reputation and giving him a reason to doubt my strength.

"We can chat later," Nora said to Nate, interrupting my string of thoughts. She stood and looped her arm around mine, steering me away from Nate and making my decision for me. "I'm sorry, that was stupid. I shouldn't be giving the crew any reason to doubt our betrothal."

"If you were to willingly choose any of our crew to be betrothed to, it would be much more believable that you'd choose Nate over me," I said. "So don't apologize."

She stopped walking and looked up at me. "I'm not here for Nate," she said matter-of-factly.

I sighed. "No. You're here because I couldn't think better on the spot to stop my father from making me kill you."

"And why did you stop your father instead of just letting him kill me himself?" she asked. "Then you wouldn't have my blood on your hands, but you'd be free to live your life, obligation free."

Obligation. That's what she thought of herself, because I'd made her think that. I wanted to correct her and tell her that I'd *wanted* her. Maybe not to be fake betrothed to, but at least to spend more time with her. In another life, one where I wasn't already darkened by my past and focused on causing my father as much grief as possible, that might have been an option. But

93

I'd only bring her down to my level, and I couldn't do that. *Wouldn't* do that.

"I don't know," I lied.

"Hmm." She slipped her arm from mine. "I'm going to lie down. I didn't get much sleep last night." And then she was gone.

I leaned my arms on the railing and stared out over the waves. Polly popped up beside me, and if I were a different man, I might have reacted. But I'd grown used to people sneaking up on me. At least I knew Polly meant no harm.

"Why are you denying yourself happiness with that girl?" she asked, her voice low. "I see how she looks at you and she'd give you the world if you asked."

I scowled. "That's ridiculous. She hates me. Maybe two days ago she might have given me a chance, but now," I paused and sighed. "I shouldn't be saying any of this." I realized I was basically admitting to Polly that my betrothal was a farce.

"You're just as stubborn as the captain," Polly said. "I don't want to watch you wither and crumble just as he has."

I swung my head to look at her. "My father has never loved another person in his life. Not even my mother."

Heaving an exasperated sigh, Polly continued. "Not your mother, no. But there was someone once. Not that he ever let her get close enough to break through that stone cold heart of his. Keep going like this, and you'll become as ugly and cruel as him."

"Good," I snapped. "I need to be cruel to be a pirate."

Patting my shoulder, Polly turned and walked away. Her touch made me squirm as my wounds ached and my body itched to shift so I could heal. But I couldn't do that. If Kerrigan

found out, he'd whip me all over again to ensure the punishment stuck.

So, I turned to my usual vice. The rum was stored on the lowest deck, and I wasn't the first one to break into a bottle for the day. A few others were shirking their duties and playing a round of cards while passing a bottle amongst them. When I arrived, they seemed to panic, but once I grabbed my own bottle and passed them by without a word, they relaxed and continued their game.

For some reason, the crew thought I was my father's spy, or something. I'd never ratted anyone out to him though. I didn't care enough to do that.

I retreated to my favorite spot, a window where a cannon used to be, where I could sit and let my legs dangle above the water. I had to slouch a little because it was a short window, but it worked.

It was the same spot I was in a few hours later when John happened upon me.

"Aeros damn me," he cursed when he came into the room, and I jumped down from the window, startling him.

"Aeros doesn't do that. Arobaras might, though." I may not believe in the gods, but sometimes I thought Arobaras, ruler of the underworld, may play a hand in my life. People often didn't speak his name for fear it would conjure him. I used it more than a few times in my life, and never once had the pleasure of meeting him.

"You're playing with fire," John warned. "Why aren't you with your betrothed? Nate will happily sweep her away if you let him."

"What's it to you?"

"I'd rather not see Nate's tongue cut out, or eyes gouged. He's too pretty for that." John smirked. I knew they were off and on, but Nate wouldn't settle for just one person. He wanted his fill, and John wouldn't deny him that.

"So long as he keeps his hands off Nora, we won't have a problem." I handed my rum bottle to John; it was still mostly full. "Enjoy."

"Nora ate dinner with Polly, but she's back in your room, now," John said. "In case you were wondering."

I kept walking, all the way to the main deck, and down to my room. Before knocking, I tested the door to make sure she'd locked it like I'd warned her to. She had. *Good girl.*

"You can open the door," I said. For a second, I thought she might be asleep. She'd taken a nap earlier, but she could still be tired. Then the door opened, and she stood there in a slip that hit mid-thigh and left nothing to the imagination.

I inhaled a sharp breath and bit my lip, trying not to stare.

She turned and lay down on the inside of the bed against the wall, leaving her back to me.

"Did I wake you?" I asked, closing and locking the door behind me.

Sighing, she turned to look at me. "No."

I removed my tunic, wincing as it shifted the bandages covering my wounds, and started to undo my belt.

"What are you doing?" she asked, her eyes widening.

"Getting ready for bed. Is that okay with you? I can always sleep on the floor again."

Turning her face back to the wall, she shrugged. "Do what you want."

"So, you're okay if I sleep naked?" I tested, watching for her reaction.

"Like I said," she said, not taking my bait.

"Hmm."

I kept my pants on and slid onto the bed behind her. Her body stiffened, but she didn't object as I pulled the light blanket up over both of us.

"What made you finally come sleep in your own room?" she asked, keeping her back to me.

"I figured people would start questioning our betrothal if I didn't sleep in here sooner or later." I winced as the blanket brushed over part of my wounds that were exposed.

"So, you're keeping up appearances." She had her arms wrapped around herself and I wondered if she was trying as hard not to touch *me* as I was not to touch *her*.

"That and the floor isn't nearly as comfortable as my bed," I said.

"Right." She was tense.

"So, what were you doing before I arrived, if you weren't sleeping?" I asked, picturing her alone in my bed, and smirked.

"Oh, um, thinking."

Reaching out, I ran my fingers through her hair. "Thinking about what, sweetheart?" I taunted.

"I'm going to bed now."

I moved closer, so I was only a breath away from being pressed against her. My hardening cock threatened to close that distance.

"It's okay to admit you were thinking about me," I said, my voice low and gravely. "I think about you often." Skimming

the tips of my fingers up her arm, goosebumps rose in their wake. "Sweet dreams, Nora."

Nora

I wasn't sure how Adrian expected me to sleep after that, but somehow, mercifully, sleep found me. But I didn't escape him in my dreams. He touched me in all the places I ached so badly for him, and when he'd finished with that, he led me to the upper deck and fucked me over the railing.

When I woke in the morning, I wasn't surprised to find myself wet from my dreams of Adrian. What I *was* surprised by was I'd rolled in my sleep and was facing him, pressed against his bare chest. His arm was draped over me and my hand ... *Oh gods.*

I pulled my hand back, accidentally stroking his hard length that I'd been practically groping in my sleep.

Adrian opened his eyes and smiled at me. He arched his back and moaned from the motion. If I hadn't already been dripping for him ...

"Good morning, sweetheart," he said. "Were you trying to grope me, or was it a happy accident?"

Heat flushed my cheeks, and I tried to move away but my back hit the wall. "I wasn't trying to do anything. You're so close, it's hard *not* to touch you."

"I am pretty irresistible." He gave me a wicked grin.

"That's not what I meant."

"Sure." He kissed my forehead and rolled away, getting out of bed.

Disappointment filled me. I wasn't sure what I wanted from Adrian, or if I wanted to be with him, but my body sure wanted him.

He pulled on his tunic and boots.

"Meet me on the main deck when you're ready," he said, leaving me behind.

As soon as the door closed, my hand drifted down between my thighs. Pulling off my undergarments, I threw them to the corner of the room and trailed my fingers up and down my slit, imagining Adrian had stayed. A small moan escaped me, and I bit my lip to remind myself to stay quiet. The walls were thin.

Though, maybe Adrian would come back if he heard me. I shook my head. More likely someone else would hear and harass me, like Gregor.

That ruined my mood, and I begrudgingly got dressed.

Adrian waited for me beside the main mast.

"Care to do some climbing?" he asked, tilting his head back and eyeing the ropes of the mast. "You said you'd spent some time on pirate ships in the past."

I furrowed my brows. "But I never checked the ropes. I wouldn't know what to do up there."

100

Adrian lifted his shoulder. "I'll do all the work. You can just enjoy the view."

"And if I fall?" I wasn't afraid of too many things, but heights were definitely on that list.

"I won't let you fall." The breeze off the water whipped around us, making his hair fall across his eyes and he swept it away.

I narrowed my eyes and put my hands on my hips. "Fine."

His eyes lit up and he grabbed the shroud attached to the mast, placing a foot on the ratline. They swung beneath his weight as he climbed. I noticed him flinch a few times and I wondered if his wounds from his lashing were bothering him, but I didn't ask. He probably didn't want to talk about that.

My heart hammered in my chest as I followed him. Jami had never let me climb the ropes when I was on his ship. I remember trying once when I was little, because it seemed fun, and I'd promptly been pulled down and scolded.

Each step I took, I thought the rope was going to give way beneath me, but none of them did. That was the point of checking the ropes; to make sure none of them were fraying or damaged.

Adrian checked the ropes as we went, and when we were high enough to see far out over the sea, we stopped. I didn't dare look down. He leaned against the ropes, letting them support his weight as he admired the sea. I clung to them and tried my best not to imagine what it would feel like falling to the deck and breaking my neck.

"Stop worrying for a second and look," Adrian said, moving so he was beside me.

101

I forced my focus to the sea and marveled at the sight. He was right, it was a decent view.

But then the ropes were moving with a gust of wind, and my fingers slipped, and I thought I'd met my end.

Adrian's hand clamped onto my wrist, and he righted me. I'd barely let go for a second, and the ropes would have held my weight fine, but it had been enough to make my life flash before my eyes.

"I'm getting down," I said, but I couldn't bring my body to move.

Adrian smirked as he watched me, waiting. "Afraid of heights?"

"No," I snapped. "Well, maybe a little."

Moving down so he was lower than me, Adrian took hold of my booted foot. I let out an embarrassing squeak of fear.

"Let me help you," he said. "I'll guide you to the next rope rung, all you have to do is lower yourself, and if you slip, I'll catch you."

Lowering my hands on the ropes that I gripped far too tightly, I let him guide my foot down and put my weight onto it. Little by little, we made our way back to the deck. We weren't nearly as high as I'd thought while up there.

Back on the much more stable deck, Adrian pulled me into his arms and kissed the top of my head.

"What was that for?" I asked, pulling away.

He kept an easy smile on his face. "People are watching, and we don't want them thinking I let you be scared without comforting you. What kind of betrothed would I be?"

Right. That's why he was being so nice.

"I wasn't scared," I said, pulling away.

"So, next time I can just leave you up there?" he teased.

"As if I'd let you drag me back up there again with that threat hanging over my head." And I didn't need another reminder so soon of my own mortality.

I drifted to the side of the ship. The sea called to me and my muscles ached to shift. I wondered if Captain Kerrigan would care if I went for a swim. It's not like I'd be leaving, but they would have to pull me back onto the ship after somehow.

"Thinking of leaving me to my fate after all?" Adrian came up beside me, placing his hand on the small of my back. Another gesture to keep up appearances.

I turned and gave him a fake smile, leaning into him.

"How far do we need to go to convince everyone this is real?" I asked, pressing my hand to his chest. I could have sworn I felt his heartbeat quicken beneath my touch. Sliding my hand up, I cupped his face and stroked my thumb over his bottom lip. "Is this too much?"

If he wanted to play with my emotions, I could play right back.

He lowered his face closer to mine, our noses practically touching. "What game are you playing, sweetheart?"

"I'm only keeping up appearances," I said innocently.

"Get a room," Nate said as he swabbed the deck nearby.

I stepped away from Adrian, feigning coyness and tucked my hair behind my ear. "Mission accomplished," I said, quiet enough for only Adrian to hear.

Adrian pawned me off on Polly again for the rest of the day, but I didn't mind. She oversaw cleaning the kitchen, so I helped her. We stopped for lunch, and Adrian sat with us

before returning to whatever his duties were. Part of me was scared to ask.

Once we finished cleaning up after lunch, Polly and I sat across from each other to rest at one of the tables.

"If you don't mind me asking, how did Adrian convince you to marry him?" Polly asked.

Putting my elbows on the table, I leaned forward. "What makes you think *he* wasn't the one who needed convincing?"

"Most women are too afraid to approach him, let alone *marry* him. I don't think he's been with a woman, who knew who he was anyway, in quite some time. Is there something you were running from in your old life?" Polly rubbed a spot on the table absentmindedly as she spoke.

I thought of my conversation with Adrian, and how I was supposed to come up with some depressing backstory to convince people that I was desperate enough to fall for him. But for some reason, I wanted to prove to these people that Adrian was worthy of love, without strings or desperation attached.

"Nothing. My old life was fine. My parents were great, until they passed away and I had to move into The Flightdeck Inn in Asmara." I figured I'd keep that part of our story, since I still needed to keep my identity hidden, and Adrian may have already told people that tale.

"Hm." Polly's hand stilled on the table. "I'm glad he found you." She hopped up and headed for the stairs.

"You coming?" she asked over her shoulder.

When we stepped onto the main deck, Captain Kerrigan eyed us from the doorway of his quarters. Locking eyes with me, he waved me over. Dread filled me.

"Good luck," Polly said, veering away.

Straightening my spine and throwing back my shoulders, I strode across the deck to meet the captain. I wouldn't let him think that he had any effect on me.

He cocked his head to the side. "A shifter like you must be itching to shift after going days without."

Panic seized me. Somehow, he knew about my lioness side.

"Being a mermaid, and all," he added, and relief washed over me.

"Oh, yes," I said, nodding like an idiot. "It gets uncomfortable after a few days, but nothing I can't handle."

Stepping forward into my space, he twisted a lock of hair that I'd left out of my braid, around his finger and leaned in too close. "That's good."

My skin was itching for a whole other reason as I forced myself not to cringe away from him. He was testing me, and I refused to back down.

"Unless you're offering to let me go for a swim," I said, smiling.

Lowering his hand back to his side and taking a step back, he waved toward the side of the ship. "You're more than welcome to, though someone may not be available to pull you back up. In which case, you'd have left Adrian behind to meet his fate because I'd think you left him, as I assumed you might."

I forced a smile. "It's a good thing I have no need to shift now. If that's all you wanted, I'll return to the tasks I was helping Polly with." I jerked my thumb over my shoulder to where I'd last seen Polly.

"Mm. As you were," he said, dismissing me as if he had any say over what I did or when I did it. Now wasn't the time to test his patience.

I backed away from him, turning to see where Polly had gone, and walked straight into Adrian.

"Oof," I huffed.

His hands gripped my elbows, steadying me. "Woah, there," he said, smirking. "In a hurry to get away from the captain?"

I glanced back, but Captain Kerrigan had retreated into his cabin. "No."

"Oh really?" He released me and took a step back. "My mistake. What were you and the captain talking about?"

I clasped my hands in front of me. "Swimming." He opened his mouth to respond, but I continued, "What have you been doing all day?"

"Helping Morgan with something."

"Hm. How vague of you," I said, rolling my eyes.

The ship rocked and I lost my footing, stumbling back into Adrian. He slipped an arm around my waist holding me in place. There were too many people around to pull away without raising questions. Though, I was sure most of them couldn't care less about me or whether I truly loved Adrian.

"Can't stay away, can you?" he teased. "I thought you said you'd been on a ship before?"

My face heated. "It's been quite a few years since I last stepped foot on a ship," I admitted. "I'll get used to it."

A small commotion started somewhere behind me and Adrian's eyes darted to it, though his expression remained stoic.

"Excuse me," he said, sidestepping me.

Adrian

"A storm's coming in," Billy said, pointing to the western horizon, where a dark cloud had appeared. "Too fast to avoid."

"Go inform the captain," I said. A few heads turned to me, surprised at my sudden appearance. "You." I pointed to Charlie, a woman who'd joined my father's crew shortly after my mother dumped me on him. "Take someone with you and start tying down the loose cargo. Cannons first. And you." I pointed to Max. "Start lowering the mainsail."

"We should be able to avoid the worst of it," Charlie said. Her short brown hair was already whipping from the wind of the incoming storm.

"Do as I say," I commanded, and she nodded before leaving the group.

"Someone should remind her to stay away from the rail," Max sniggered.

I glanced over at Nora, standing with her elbows propped on the railing as she watched the storm rolling in.

"She's a mermaid, you idiot," Billy said. "If she falls in, she'll just shift."

107

I rolled my eyes and left the crew members behind, striding toward Nora.

"Beautiful, isn't it?" she asked.

"Ah yes. The bane of every sailor's existence. Absolutely breathtaking." My voice was thick with sarcasm.

She sighed. "You don't get it." Pushing off the railing, she headed for the stairs.

"Where are you going?" I asked, my gaze following her.

"I won't be of any use in the storm, so I'm getting out of the way. Is that okay with you?" She continued down the stairs without waiting for my answer.

A part of me wanted to follow her and ride out the storm locked away in our room. But if my father found out, I'd risk another lashing. Normally that wouldn't deter me, but my wounds were still too fresh and deep.

"Adrian." *Think of the man and he shall appear.* I groaned inwardly. Kerrigan exited his room and headed straight for me. His gaze skipped over me to the horizon, and he narrowed his eyes at the storm. "It'll barely cause an issue," he said.

"I hope you're right, but if not, I've got the crew preparing." I always liked to get on top of things before we were in the thick of a storm. There'd been one too many close calls in the past, and my father tended to underprepare every time.

"You don't normally take command in these situations." He sucked his teeth. "Could it be you're concerned for the wellbeing of your betrothed?"

I opened my mouth to make a snarky response, but a lightning strike in the distance distracted me.

"Mermaids can swim, Adrian, lest you forgot. It should be yourself and my crew you're worrying about," Kerrigan said.

"I'm not worried about her. She's safely stowed away in our room, probably napping for all she cares about this storm," I argued. But now that he'd mentioned it, there was a small nagging worry deep in the pit of my stomach, and I couldn't help but wonder if maybe I *was* worried about her, despite knowing she'd be fine if our entire ship went down.

"Good. Like I said, this storm won't cause us any issues. We'll likely miss it entirely."

"Then you don't need me on deck," I pointed out. "I can retire to my cabin to be with Nora." I was testing him, pushing him to admit that this storm might turn out to be something more than what he'd claimed. But he would never admit he was wrong.

He waved a hand toward the stairs. "Be my guest. Shirk your duties and attend to the woman. I'm sure the crew has the preparations well in hand."

"Right." I smirked and made my way to the stairs, half expecting my father to stop me, but he didn't.

Forgetting that I'd told Nora to lock the door whenever she was alone in our room, I tried to open it without knocking.

"Who is it?" she called through the door.

I almost walked away. She would probably prefer it if I left her alone.

Instead, I knocked and said, "It's me, sweetheart."

Every time I waited for her to open the door for me, anticipation built, and it was almost as if I was seeing her for the first time again. Struck by her beauty as she stared up at me in the doorway.

"Are you just going to stand there?" she asked, backing away from the door and plopping down onto the bed, and crossing her legs out in front of her. She'd taken her hair out of the braid and had it all brushed to one side. I wanted to run my hands through it and grip it while I pulled her head back and ...

"Adrian?" She cocked one of her eyebrows and leaned forward, resting her arms over one slightly bent knee.

My cock twitched. *Gods.* She was going to be my undoing.

"Aren't you supposed to be helping prepare for the storm?" she asked.

I cleared my throat and stepped into the room, closing the door behind me. "According to Captain Kerrigan, we should be able to avoid the storm. So, I'm not needed on deck."

"So that means I don't really need to stay down here then," she said. "Unless ..." She trailed off and leaned back against the pillows.

"Unless?" I asked, taking a step forward and lifting my knee to prop it on the end of the bed.

Nora's gaze traveled down to where my cock strained against my pants, and she bit her bottom lip.

It was taking every ounce of restraint not to move further onto the bed and bury myself inside her. I didn't want to take more than she wanted to offer.

"I—"

Someone banged on the door, interrupting me, and I whipped around to throw it open.

"What?" I growled, clearly scaring Billy who stood on the other side, cowering.

"S—sorry, sir. Captain sent me to fetch you. You're needed behind the helm."

I ground my jaw. I should have known that my father would never actually let me off the hook for this storm. No matter that he thought we'd avoid the worst of it. He'd let me come down here, thinking I'd have time with Nora, and yanked me back right as things were about to get interesting. He was playing with fire.

"Hold tight, sweetheart," I said as I left the room. "I'll be back as soon as we're clear of this storm."

Rain had made the deck slick, and it took extra effort to keep myself on my feet as I made my way to the helm. Morgan was already there, holding the wheel as steady as she could despite the waves trying to move us off course.

"I was informed I was needed for this job," I told her, yelling slightly to be heard over the chaos of the storm.

Morgan stepped aside, letting me take over, but she remained close, almost like she wanted to say something.

Glancing over at her as the rungs threatened to pull from my hands, I asked, "What's bothering you now?"

Her gaze darted to me and narrowed momentarily, before she turned on her heel and strode for the stairs.

Ever since I'd been left on my father's ship, she'd been that way. Never revealing her emotions, never saying too many words, and never letting anyone close enough to truly know her. But somehow, I felt like I *did* know her.

Morgan was the one who took my hand and led me into Kerrigan's quarters that first night when my mother shoved me off her and onto the hard deck. I'd been clinging to her leg,

afraid of the pirates who stared from all around. No one dared approach, except for Morgan.

"Adrian is Kerrigan's problem now," my mother had said. *"Let him deal with the boy and raise him."*

That was when her leather bracelet, that was now strapped around my wrist, had either fallen or she'd dropped it for me. I liked to think she wanted me to have something to remember her by, but that was a fool's hope.

After taking my hand and pulling me to my feet, Morgan had snapped, "Never let the enemy see you cry." Then she half dragged me to Kerrigan's quarters and explained to him what had happened.

At first, Kerrigan was dead set on throwing me overboard and letting me drown, but Morgan was the one who noticed my snake fangs, which always came out on their own when I had any kind of strong emotion as a child. She pointed out that Kerrigan could use my venom to help him carry out King Danforth's tasks, which usually involved quietly murdering any threat to his reign.

That was the only time Morgan ever stepped in to save me from harm.

The wheel jerked from my grasp, but I quickly grabbed hold of it again and steadied it, wiping the rain from my eyes. There were clearer skies not too far off, and I hated to admit that Kerrigan had been right. The storm wouldn't be a problem for much longer.

As the rain slowed and the sky lightened, all I could think about was getting back to Nora.

Nora

I'd had to take care of myself after Adrian left. He'd had me gripping the sheets with anticipation before Billy knocked on the door and shattered our moment. It hadn't quelled my thrumming need for release.

It had been hours since he'd left and we'd only hit a few large waves that had sent a couple loose items rolling across the floor, but as Captain Kerrigan had guessed, the storm wasn't too serious.

When someone knocked on the door, I was expecting Adrian, so I opened it without asking who it was. *Stupid.*

Instead, Captain Kerrigan stood there wearing a calculating smile. "Join me for a moonlit stroll?" he asked, holding his hand out to me.

I hadn't realized how long I'd been in that room for, but when we made it to the main deck, the moon shone down through the remaining clouds and crew members were playing cards across the way. The rain had left the deck slick, so I stepped carefully.

"This way." Captain Kerrigan had released my hand almost immediately after me taking it earlier, but then he'd put his hand on my lower back to guide me, which might have been worse.

Up the stairs and past the helm, which Adrian was no longer at, to the back of the ship we went. There were a few people there when we arrived, but Captain Kerrigan gave them some indication they needed to leave, and they did. I almost wanted to scream for help, even though he'd done nothing to indicate he meant me harm. *Yet.*

"I understand that you care for my son. However, I also understand that you have never quite seen him in the light that I have," Captain Kerrigan said, leaning one arm on the railing.

"I've seen more of him than you might think," I retorted, thinking of that first night we'd met, and he'd danced with me.

Captain Kerrigan pursed his lips, and I knew I'd irked him by speaking out of turn.

"He probably hasn't told you how many men he's killed, or how many of his own crew he's maimed. You may think me cruel for what happened the other night, but Adrian has doled out the same punishment on many occasions."

Goosebumps rose on my skin despite the warm air. I ran a hand over my arm, trying to make them disappear.

"Why are you telling me all of this?" I asked, my voice betraying my discomfort.

"I want to give you the opportunity to change your mind. You're a mermaid, you can leave now, and he'll never have to know why." He looked out to the sea before returning his focus to me.

"You said you'd kill him if I disappeared," I reminded him.

"I'm a fair man. If you leave now, I promise I won't kill him. Though, I will have to make an example of him somehow, just so no one thinks I went back on my word. You understand." Lifting a hand, he gripped my arm for a few seconds before releasing me and wiping his hand on the hem of his coat.

I glanced out over the water, considering his offer. Being stuck on this ship for a week with a bunch of pirates I didn't know wasn't ideal. And I wouldn't have Adrian's death hanging over me if I left. My body itched to shift as if it sensed the decision I was so close to making.

But I'd made a promise to Adrian to stick with him until he came up with his own way for me to leave. A way that wouldn't endanger him.

Morgan's words came back to me. *You may be betrothed to Adrian, but you know nothing of the things he has endured on this ship at Captain Kerrigan's hand and behest.*

I wouldn't be the cause of one more thing he would have to endure because of his father.

"I'm not leaving him, Captain." I kept my response plain and simple. I didn't need him reading into it or finding a way to twist my words.

His eyebrows rose in surprise. "Well. I guess I should be happy that my son has found such a devoted partner."

Footsteps moved toward us at a quick pace and relief washed over me when Adrian stepped out of the shadows.

"Captain, what's going on?" He looked me over before moving to my side and placing his hand on my lower back. "Anything you say to my betrothed you can say in front of me."

"Well, if you truly care to know, I was giving Nora here a chance to change her mind. We all know the man you truly are, and I would hate for a woman like her to be walking blindly into a life with you without having someone give her a way out."

Adrian's hand at my back stiffened though his expression didn't change.

"You'll be happy to know she turned me down." Captain Kerrigan turned on his heel and strode toward the stairs, but he stopped right before going down and glanced back at us. "We may as well perform your wedding right on this ship, seeing as you two are so clearly infatuated with one another. It will give the crew a pick me up."

"Father," Adrian started, but Captain Kerrigan put his hand up.

"No need to thank me. I've always wanted to perform a wedding ceremony since becoming a captain."

"Bull shit," Adrian muttered, too low for Captain Kerrigan to hear.

When the captain had gone, I turned to Adrian and said, "I don't know why he did that."

Adrian didn't move or blink. I wasn't even sure if he was breathing.

I continued, "He said he'd let me go and not kill you if I left now."

"Why didn't you go?" Adrian asked, taking his hand from my back. He paced the deck. "That was your out! That was your chance to leave without consequences. Now we have to go through with this betrothal."

I blinked rapidly, confused. I stupidly thought he'd be *happy* I stayed. Or at least grateful. Not angry.

"Not without consequences," I said the first thing that came to my mind. "Not without consequences," I repeated a little quieter. For some reason it was the *only* thing on my mind.

"He'd have me lashed again, or bled out to the brink of death, or some stupid punishment, but we'd be free of this betrothal. You could go home." He stopped pacing. "That was stupid, Nora."

That made me snap. I ran at him, shoving him as hard as I could, and he stumbled.

"How dare you! I am *not* stupid. Maybe naïve, maybe too trusting, too caring, too ... I don't know! But I'm. Not. Stupid. And I am tired of hearing it." I started to walk away but then I got a second wind and whirled back to him. " *You're* stupid!" I felt like a child yelling at him like that, but I didn't care.

" *You* danced with me that night, and *you* bought me the dagger, and *you* started this whole betrothal—" I stopped, realizing the whole ship could probably hear me. "Your father was right and you're not the man I thought you were. But I don't regret staying. Maybe you think violence isn't a consequence, but to me it is. And it's not stupid for me to think that, or to believe that you might have cared about me. But clearly you don't, so I'll stay in the room and out of your way as much as possible until we arrive in Lanteria."

As much as I hoped Adrian wasn't responding because I'd finally gotten through to him, I assumed he was just thinking about how stupid I was again.

"Nora, wait." For the first time since I'd met him, Adrian sounded unsure.

I paused, my foot hovering over the stairs I'd been about to descend. When I turned and saw him approaching me, I backed against the rail and waited.

"What now?" I asked, exhausted from my outpouring of emotion.

He'd closed the distance between us and brought a hand up to the back of my neck, digging into my hair, the other on my waist. His lips were inches from my own, but he stayed hovering there.

"I shouldn't do this," he said, his gaze flicking between my mouth and my eyes. "Tell me to stop."

"Why?" I asked, breathless from his proximity. I didn't wait for his answer. Instead, I wound my arms behind his neck and pulled him down, closing the distance, and kissing him. He tasted like rum, which made me pull back. "Are you drunk?" I asked.

Grinning, he kissed me again before pulling away. His arms stayed around me, but now I was leaning against the railing. "Hardly."

"Is that the only reason you're kissing me? Because I don't want you waking up in the morning regretting this."

"I'm not drunk, sweetheart. But don't worry, I won't regret this tomorrow, or the day after that, or the day after that, or—"

I kissed him to shut him up. He leaned in closer, pressing against me and bending me back over the railing.

"This wasn't how I imagined you bending me over the railing," I murmured between kisses.

Adrian stiffened and I straightened, biting my lower lip.

"You've been thinking about that, have you?" he asked, brushing his thumb over my jaw. "Because I'd be happy to bring that daydream to life if that's what you want."

"I—I mean, someone might see." I panicked. I'd never done anything like that before, and I didn't know how serious he was.

He ran a hand down my hair, cupping my cheek. "Don't worry, sweetheart, we won't do anything you aren't ready for." He kissed me softly. "Come on, let's see if there's any food left in the galley. I'm starved." His arm curved around my waist as we took the stairs to the main deck. He switched so quickly from passionate to casual, but I was still hot and breathless.

A few of the crew glanced our way, but no one said anything. We'd been so close to the stairs; they probably saw everything. Heat flamed my cheeks, and I tucked closer to Adrian's side.

"Don't worry, they expect us to kiss. We are betrothed after all," he teased.

There were a few others still in the galley, but Adrian and I sat in our corner alone with the slop of the day in our bowls.

We ate in silence, and I wondered if whatever mood had caused our moment on the upper deck had passed and Adrian regretted his choice to kiss me after all.

He finished his food and cleared his throat. "I'm sorry," he said, taking me by surprise.

Setting my bowl down, I wiped my hands nervously on my leggings. "For what?"

"For calling you stupid. I didn't mean it like that."

I sighed in relief. "Oh, that. I'll forgive you, but don't let it happen again." I stuck my tongue out and scrunched my nose at him, making him laugh.

"And I'll forgive you for calling *me* stupid," he said.

I shook my head. "Oh no, I meant it when I said that."

"Oh really? Well, I probably deserved it."

Standing and taking my hand, he led me up the stairs. We passed the crew playing cards and headed for the stairs down to the crew's quarters.

Before we made it, Gregor yelled across the deck, "I was beginning to think I'd have to fuck her for you."

I kept a death grip on Adrian's hand, but he whirled back to face Gregor.

"All alone in that room every night, I can only imagine how lonely she was, and everywhere she touched herself." Gregor kept talking despite Adrian taking steps back across the deck, practically dragging me behind him.

"Adrian," I warned. His hand slipped from mine, and he was on top of Gregor, the chair smashing beneath their weight. Gregor lay flat on his back, sneering up at Adrian who straddled him.

The rest of the crew jumped to their feet, excited about the action.

Adrian's arm pressed against Gregor's throat, pinning him in place, while Gregor laughed soundlessly.

No one attempted to pull them apart, and I didn't dare get any closer. Adrian had pulled a knife from somewhere and held the sharpened edge against Gregor's mouth between his teeth, digging into the corners and drawing blood.

"I'll give you the choice of your tongue or an eye," Adrian growled.

Gregor spit and it hit Adrian in the eye.

"Good choice." Adrian moved the knife to Gregor's left eye and began carving it from his face.

I couldn't watch. Running to the side of the ship, I vomited over the rail. Part of me wanted to jump over, shift, and leave. But I stayed, knees to chest and head resting on them, hyperventilating.

Someone came over and helped me to my feet, handing me a cup of water. Polly, of course.

"Come, dear, let's get you out of here." She kept her arm around my shoulders and led me to my room, sitting with me on the bed and rubbing my back as my breathing slowly returned to normal.

"Does he do that often?" I asked when I found my voice.

Polly stopped rubbing my back and clasped her hands in her lap. "I'm not going to lie to you, because you should know what you're getting yourself into."

"Now you're starting to sound like Captain Kerrigan," I huffed, a nervous laugh escaping me.

"The difference is, I don't mean to hurt Adrian by telling you this. I just want to help you understand. Adrian hurts people because he doesn't know any other way. It sounds absurd, coming from me." Polly picked at the blanket, not looking me in the eye.

"Because you're a pirate?" I asked.

"Because I've hurt my fair share of people too. But also, yes, because I'm a pirate. Adrian thinks that he must prove

121

himself, to the crew and his father, and to Morgan." Sighing, Polly shook her head.

"Why Morgan? I understand wanting to make his father proud, no matter how horrible he is." It was something I assumed all children wanted at some point, though Captain Kerrigan was one of the less deserving parents of that sentiment.

"Morgan helped make him into the man he is. She trained him to maim and kill. She's the one who finds him whenever he's taken by other crews, or people with vendettas against Captain Kerrigan. But she waits until he fights his way out, as if she's making him stronger or something. It's a twisted game for them, Morgan and the captain that is. Adrian just goes along with it." The anger was written on Polly's face. She *hated* Morgan for what she did to Adrian.

Putting my hand on Polly's shoulder, I asked, "Why are you telling me this? Adrian is so convinced that no one cares about him, but you seem to care."

"I've seen too many people go the way Adrian's going. His own father being one of them. I don't want Adrian to end up like him."

I studied Polly a little more closely. "Why are you a pirate?" I asked, hoping I wasn't being too bold.

"You ask as if you don't already know." Her gaze drifted to the ceiling as if she might see through it to the man she once cared about.

"You loved Captain Kerrigan once, didn't you?" I guessed. From the way she talked about who he once was, it almost seemed like she may have hope that the man she once loved was still in there. But I had no hope for him.

She pursed her lips. "And yet I'm still here."

"I'm sorry." I was so used to seeing the people around me *stay* with the loves of their lives. Even Lia and Jami made it work long distance. It was a bit unsettling to see how things could go so wrong. I wanted to cry for Polly, but I figured she'd resent that.

"Don't be. I chose to stay, and now it's as if we never happened." She stood and went to the doorway. "I should go see how things have unfolded."

"Can you tell Adrian that I'll wait up for him? If you see him."

Polly smiled. "Of course." She closed the door, and I locked it behind her.

And then I waited.

And waited.

Until, about two hours later, a knock on the door had me jolting upright.

"It's me, sweetheart."

Adrian

I expected Nora to ignore me and keep the door locked all night. Except she didn't. The door creaked open, and she looked at me like she had before. Before I'd carved out Gregor's eye in front of her. And it nearly sent me to my knees with relief.

"Are you done?" she asked, and I cocked my head in confusion. "Are you done being stupid?" Her smile made me weak, and I pushed the door open fully, stepping into the room.

"You think you're funny," I said, kicking the door shut behind me as she backed up, her legs hitting the bed. "Don't you, sweetheart?"

"As a matter of fact, I do," she said, scrunching her nose and sticking her tongue out at me, like she'd done before.

I ran my fingers up and down her arms, feeling goosebumps rise in the wake of my touch. Her hands drifted over my shoulders, and she leaned into me.

Despite her words, she trembled slightly, and I worried she was hiding her fear. Her fear of me and what I'd done.

"You don't need to pretend with me," I said. "I'd understand if you had changed your mind ..."

124

Pulling back, she furrowed her brow as she looked up at me. "I'm not changing my mind, and I'm not pretending."

"Any sane person might have cause to be afraid," I pointed out.

"So, you're calling me insane now?" she teased, the tip of her pinky tracing a line beneath my lower lip.

Smiling, I pressed my forehead against hers. "Can you blame me? I'm not exactly someone who deserves attention from someone like you."

"Watch your mouth. That's my *betrothed* your talking about." Her hands moved to my shoulders, pushing me lightly. "I'm choosing this. I'm choosing *you.*" Leaning forward, she kissed me lightly.

I kissed her softly at first, before moving her down onto the bed. Her hair splayed around her like a halo. I propped myself above her, staring at her while she gazed up at me.

"What?" she asked, breathless.

"I was just thinking about how beautiful you are. And how I should have done this sooner." I smirked and ducked down to press my lips against the side of her throat. I made a trail down to where her corset began, and she writhed beneath me.

Her hands moved from my shoulders and her nails dug into my back. Hissing in pain, I clenched my jaw and tried not to drop my weight on top of her. It had only been two days since my lashing and my wounds were still raw.

"Oh my gods!" she cried. "I forgot about your back! I am so sorry!" Her eyes were wide open, and her hands cupped my face.

I cursed my wounds for not healing faster and for ruining the moment. Rolling onto my side, I sat on the edge of the bed, turning to face her.

"Why didn't you shift to heal the wounds?" she asked, concern pinching her features.

"The last time I made that mistake I was twelve and my father had me lashed twice as many times to make up for the ones I'd healed. He said if I shifted and healed after being lashed, I wouldn't get the full effect of the punishment. It would make me weak and spineless, and he wouldn't tolerate that."

Instead of saying she was sorry, or taking pity on me, she sat up and reached toward me.

"Here, let me see," she said, scooting closer and pulling at the hem of my tunic.

"I don't want to make you sick again," I said, holding my tunic down.

She sighed and rolled her eyes. "That was different. I wasn't expecting that." Moving to kneel beside me, she tugged on my tunic again. "Trust me."

I caved and put my arms up so she could remove my tunic. She inhaled sharply and her fingertips brushed featherlight along the edges of my wounds that were visible from under my poor wrapping.

"Would your father notice if you shifted and healed just a little? Just enough so that they don't get infected?" she asked.

"I've never risked that, but I'm sure he won't look at them until the next time, and by then he'll have expected me to shift. Unless I piss him off tomorrow."

"Right," she sighed.

I jerked in surprise as she pressed her lips to my shoulder, and she laughed.

"Do these lines mean anything?" she asked as she traced one of my tattoos on my shoulder, down my arm.

"No. It just reminded me of waves, and I liked it, so I got it." Most of my tattoos were meaningless.

"And this?" Her fingertip brushed along my hip. I had a sunrise there.

"Again, I just liked it," I said, trying not to move as she kept exploring. My cock strained against my trousers, and I wanted to finish what we'd started, but she seemed content, and I didn't want to push her.

"Want to see mine?" she whispered in my ear, and my restraint almost left me.

I turned my head and captured her lips with mine.

"Is that a yes?" She backed away, rocking from her knees onto her butt and stretched her legs out in front of her. "Help me out of these."

When I didn't move immediately, she started the work herself, shimmying the tight fabric down her legs. I hopped in and finished the job for her, throwing the leggings into the corner of the room. That's when I saw her tattoo right below her hipbone, almost concealed by her undergarments. It was small, maybe the size of my thumb, and I had to get closer to figure out what it was.

It was a mermaid tail.

"So I always have my tail, even when I'm out of the water," she explained. "And I just liked it." She winked.

"Hm." I lowered my mouth to her inner thigh, protracting my snake fangs. "Do you trust me?" I asked.

127

Her throat bobbed and she nodded.

I dragged my fangs lightly along her inner thigh and then used them to rip off her undergarments.

She shuddered beneath me, and I inched toward her center.

"Adrian," she warned, and I paused. "Don't stop."

I huffed a laugh and continued my exploration, teasing her with my thumb and forefinger. She was already slick with desire. Impatient, she dug her hands into my hair, urging me closer to her core. I obliged, running my tongue up the center of her and letting my fangs graze her sensitive peak.

"Oh gods," she moaned.

My tongue and fingers moved in a rhythm, working to bring her to ruin.

I slid my hand up her torso to her mouth so she could bite me instead of letting her pleasure be known to the whole ship. The pain centered me as she bit down hard on the edge of my hand.

Extricating myself from her legs which had wrapped around my neck, I moved up to kiss her and pressed my hard length against her, moaning into her mouth.

Blood smeared her lips from where one of my fangs had sliced her and I sucked it off, retracting my fangs. I tasted no hint of my venom. It wouldn't be a problem unless I truly bit her.

Her hands worked at my pants, attempting to untie them, but her attention was divided between that task and kissing me, so she was making no progress.

"Let me help with that," I murmured, pushing myself up and off the bed. I made quick work of untying and removing my pants.

Nora licked her lips as she watched me. When I'd finished undressing, she sat up turning her back to me.

"Me next," she said, casting a sensual look over her shoulder as she waited for me to untie her corset. It took me a little longer than my pants, but I got the thing untied and dropped it to the side of the bed.

Laying back, she bared herself to me fully and I let my gaze rake over her, taking her in.

"Beautiful, sweetheart." I positioned myself over her again and her hands went to my arms and my shoulders, but never strayed to my back.

My hands roamed everywhere as I knelt over her. Up her thighs, over her hips, to her breasts, and into her hair.

"You're being mean," she said, moving her hands to my thighs and making my cock twitch.

"You're right." I grinned, leaning down and kissing her.

She gripped my length between us and lined it up with her entrance and as I pressed into her, she let out a low hiss. I paused and ran my thumb over her temple.

"Alright?" I asked.

She bucked her hips in response, taking me deeper inside. It was my turn to hiss from the ecstasy of being inside her.

She crushed her mouth to mine, swiping her tongue inside and biting my bottom lip.

I thrusted in time with her movements, until she couldn't keep up and I took over. Her palm pressed flat against my chest, and as her nails dug into me, I knew she was close to finishing.

Putting one of my hands to her mouth again, I had to keep my weight on one arm.

"Bite as hard as you need to, sweetheart," I told her between thrusts.

"Mmmm," she moaned in response, the vibration tickling my hand.

When she came, she bit down hard enough to draw blood.

"Oh gods." Her voice was muffled, and I removed my hand from her mouth, finishing myself off with a few more thrusts.

I drowned my own moans in her mouth as I kissed her again and collapsed on top of her, my arm finally giving out on me.

Rolling to the side, she rolled with me, keeping me inside her.

"Sorry about your hand," she said sheepishly. Her own hands were fisted and pressed against my chest.

"You hardly did any damage." I held it between us and showed her the marks. "Besides, I like having this reminder of what just occurred." Gripping her thigh, I pulled her leg up over my hip and leaned forward to kiss her. My cock throbbed inside her as if it wouldn't take much for me to be ready for round two.

She ground her hips against me, and her kisses became more desperate, like she couldn't get enough. I knew exactly how she felt. I moved my mouth to her peaked nipples, giving

them each a nibble, before sucking one into my mouth and flicking it with my tongue.

Nora moaned and her pussy clenched around me.

One of her hands tangled in my hair while the other roamed lower, grazing my balls and making me harden inside of her. I moved slowly, pumping in and out of her, letting her moans escalate, until I covered her mouth again.

She nipped at my hand playfully, so I replaced it with my lips, swallowing her moans.

When Nora started to pull away, I got worried I'd hurt her somehow, but after my cock slid out of her, she moved to the edge of the bed and pulled me to follow her.

"I'd have you lie on your back, but." She shrugged and knelt beside the bed, and I realized what she was doing.

Standing up, I held my breath as she ran her tongue up the length of my cock and began stroking it. Her mouth closed around the end of it, and she took me in slowly at first.

I fisted my hand in her hair as she used her hand to pump me and took the rest of my length into her mouth.

Throwing my head back, I bit my fist to stifle my groans as she moved faster and took me deeper. It didn't take long before I came, and I relished the sight of her swallowing it.

I helped her to her feet and kissed her before we both collapsed back on the bed, me on my side and her back pressed against my chest. Wrapping my arm around her, I held her close.

"We're more than halfway to Lanteria," I mused. That meant Nora only had to endure being on Kerrigan's ship for another couple days and hopefully we could find a way for her to return safely home soon after.

"Mmm." She sounded like she might be falling asleep.

"If my father finds the girl he's looking for, maybe we'll be able to go right back to Asmara," I said.

Nora stiffened and craned her head to look at me.

"The girl he's looking for?" she asked. I thought I heard fear in her voice, but then again, it may be exhaustion.

"Some kid of some enemy he used to have. Apparently, she might be able to shift into two different forms because she was born to two different shifters," I explained.

"Impossible," she muttered, turning her face away again. Her finger ran beneath the leather bracelet on my wrist. "Who is Elise?"

"My mother." The words came out a bit more vehemently than I'd meant. "Were you worried I had another betrothed out there somewhere?" I teased, trying to lighten the mood once more.

Turning in my arms, Nora faced me and kissed me.

"What's this from?" she asked when she'd pulled away, tracing the scar beside my left eye.

I took her hand and brought it to my lips.

"My father threw something at me when I was younger and pissed him off. I'm good at that." I smirked, but Nora frowned.

"I hate your father for what he's done to you," she said. "Fathers are supposed to keep you safe, not cause you harm."

"Mm, sorry sweetheart, but that's often not the case. Especially among pirates."

She shook her head. "My father would never—" Stopping abruptly, her eyes widened. "I mean, like you said. My parents are dead as far as anyone here knows."

"But that's *my* story for you. I want to know the truth about you. Tell me something no one else knows." I ran a hand down her arm, and she shivered.

"Well, you know that I'm a mermaid," she started, biting her lip as she paused, and I nodded for her to go on. "But I didn't grow up in Thalassia like most do. I only recently was able to stay there for two years to decide if it's where I wanted to live permanently."

"And?" I asked. I figured I knew the answer since she wasn't there.

"And it wasn't home for me. Something was missing." She traced the lines of my tattoos with the tip of her pinky.

"Lucky for me," I said.

"Your turn. Tell me something about you that no one else knows." Her gaze lifted to mine, her tracing stopping and her hand splaying on my chest.

"You've already seen more of me than anyone else ever has," I admitted. It was the truth, and it terrified me. "So please, go easy on me."

She laughed and it was the most amazing sound I'd ever heard.

"*You're* the one who needs to go easy on *me*." She kissed me gently.

I held her tight, thinking to myself, *you don't know how wrong you are.*

133

Nora

I'd expected Adrian to at least be in the room when I woke the next morning, but he was gone. Curling in on myself for a few minutes, I considered what that meant.

Maybe he regretted what we'd done. Maybe he decided he'd had enough of me. Maybe it didn't mean to him what it meant to me. Maybe ... maybe I was overthinking everything and he'd simply been called away in the early morning.

Get hold of yourself, I chided myself and got out of bed.

I wasn't about to sulk in bed while Adrian did ... whatever he did. As Adrian had said, we still had a couple of days on the ship and there were far more productive things I could be doing. Polly couldn't be the only decent person out of the whole crew. I'd spend some time figuring out who I could trust in case I needed help with anything.

After dressing, I took the contraceptive tonic I'd had the forethought to pack and slipped out the door, scanning the bunks to see if anyone remained. A few people were sleeping in the hammocks, probably some of the ones who had been up all night.

I took the steps carefully, trying not to wake anyone or draw attention to myself. There were too many crew members I would hate to be caught alone with.

On the main deck, there were a couple of people hanging around near the doors to Captain Kerrigan's quarters. They looked like they were pretending to be busy, but it was clear they were straining to hear whatever was happening in that room.

Walking over to Nate, I asked him, "What's going on?"

He leaned on the mop he'd been swabbing the deck with and jerked his head to the door. "Captain and Adrian have been going at it since I came up here."

I scrunched my nose. "About what?"

Scratching his chin, Nate shrugged and said, "Well, *you.*"

Polly came up on my other side and put her hand on my shoulder. "I'm sure he means nothing by it," she said, as if I knew what the fuck she was talking about.

Moving closer to the door, I caught a few words.

"It's not right. I don't care what you do to me, don't make me marry her on this ship," Adrian said.

It felt like cold water had been dumped on me. He was arguing with the captain to try and get out of marrying me, as if it was such a terrible fate. He still had to keep up pretenses though, so he wouldn't outright say he didn't want to marry me.

"Said you wouldn't want to be married on a ship in front of a bunch of pirates you didn't know," Nate said. "I don't blame you."

"It's not that," I said, but I didn't know why I bothered. These people wouldn't think twice about me once I was gone.

They hardly cared whether I got *married* in front of them. The only one who cared was Captain Kerrigan because he saw it as a punishment for Adrian. A way to manipulate him and prove a point.

Steering me away from the captain's quarters, Polly led me to the stairs. "Let's get some food."

I didn't protest. My stomach was growling, and it was hard not to think about why I was much hungrier that morning.

Whatever meat we ate was flavorless and tough, but it filled me up enough to stop the discomfort. I was grateful that Polly didn't try to talk to me because I was too lost in my own thoughts to focus on a conversation.

If Adrian wanted to be rid of me so badly, maybe I *should* have taken the captain up on his offer. I could be home in my own bed. *But then I'd be right back where I started. Longing for freedom.*

Sighing, I pushed my empty bowl away and dropped my head onto my arms on the table.

"Has Adrian ever brought another girl onto the ship before?" I asked, my words coming out muffled.

Polly chuckled. "Never. He's never even *mentioned* any other women around me, or Nate and we're the closest thing he has to friends on this ship."

"Why do I feel like I've fallen for some kind of scheme? Like, *pretend you're betrothed until you get her to fuck you and then convince your father to kick her off the ship.*"

Patting my hand, Polly sighed. "That's not what's happening, Nora. Trust me, whatever Adrian is trying to get the captain to agree to is for your benefit."

"We'll see," I grumbled.

The bench I sat on creaked as someone sat beside me.

"Shows over," a feminine voice said. "Adrian stormed out of the captain's quarters and disappeared somewhere belowdecks."

I glanced over my arm and a woman with short brown hair, like my mother's, and dark brown eyes stared at me, pity in her gaze.

"I'd steer clear of him for a while," she said.

"Which one? Adrian or the captain?" I asked.

"Both. It's been a while since they had an argument of that stature. Usually Adrian defies the captain, the captain disciplines him, and then it's over. They don't argue like they did this morning."

I tucked my head back into my arms and muttered, "That's reassuring."

"I'm Charlie, by the way. Don't think we officially met." She didn't try to shake my hand, which I was grateful for.

"Nora," I said, not bothering to lift my head.

Despite what Charlie said, I was going to find Adrian. I needed answers. If he didn't want anything to do with me, that was fine, but I wanted to make sure we were on the same page, so I didn't keep throwing myself at him and embarrassing myself.

Pushing up from the table, I rolled my shoulders and headed for the crew's quarters. I'd check our room first, and if he wasn't there, then I'd check with the rum. Something told me that an argument with his father might drive him into the rum barrels. I wouldn't mind a drink myself.

"Where might one find the rum on this ship?" I asked.

137

Charlie chuckled. "Don't worry, I'll keep you busy enough you'll forget all about your problems. Then, when we've reached a more acceptable time for rum, according to the captain anyway, I'll show you where the best of it is kept."

I threw my plan to find Adrian out the window and nodded eagerly. If I could avoid him for a while, maybe I could think up the perfect thing to say to him when I saw him again. Something that would even the score.

Clapping a hand on my shoulder, Charlie headed toward the stairs. "Come on."

I followed her to the upper deck, surprised when she stepped up to the man at the helm and told him we were taking over.

Once he was gone, I said, "I've never been at the helm before."

Charlie put a hand on the helm, leaning against it as she studied me. "I'm sure there's a lot you've never done before, Kid."

Kid. I scrunched my nose at the title. I was far from a child, and she didn't look all that much older than me. But to her, I probably seemed like a clueless kid.

"Right now, with the minimal wind and waves, this is probably the easiest job we could be doing. All we have to do is make sure we stay on course," she explained. "Here." She handed me a compass. "Keep an eye on that and make sure we maintain the direction of North Northeast."

Looking down at the compass, I pinpointed the red arrow that indicated North.

"We're on course," I said. "Now what?"

"You can hold this." She stepped back and waved to the wheel. "Put a hand here, and here."

I did as she said and held the helm so that it remained steady. Every so often, it would jerk from a wave or try to lean a little one way or the other.

"This seems like it could become quite boring after a while," I pointed out.

"That's why there's more than one of us who know how to man the helm. The captain does it sometimes, too. But we trade out, so we don't lose our minds from staring too long at the wheel and the ocean."

"How long have you been a pirate?" I asked, loosening my grip on the wheel so I didn't strain myself too hard.

"All my life. My father was a pirate, and my mother died a few years after I was born, so he took me out on the ship with him."

We chatted for a while about our lives, most of what I shared was true, except for the fact I had to lie about my parents' identities. By the time someone came to replace us at the helm, I'd almost forgotten about Adrian's slight that morning. *Almost.*

It was midafternoon when we went to lunch and most of the food was already gone. Thankfully Charlie had some sway with whoever ran the kitchen that day and got us two bowls of slop. It was cold and barely edible, but it filled my stomach.

"Thank you for doing this," I said once we'd finished eating.

"What?" Charlie cocked her eyebrow and pushed her empty bowl aside. "Getting you food?"

"Well, yes, that, but also for teaching me something new. And keeping me busy. I appreciate it and am glad not to be

pestering Polly yet again. I think she needs a break from me." I laughed softly.

"I don't mind. When you live on a pirate ship, you crave change sometimes. You provided that for me today, so I should be thanking you." Taking both of our bowls, she dropped them into the wash bin. "Ready for me to show you where we keep the rum?" She pumped her eyebrows and jerked her head to the door beside the stairs.

I nodded and followed her through the door, leading to another small set of stairs that brought us down to the cargo hold. Nate and Billy and another man I hadn't met were already there, playing a game of cards and passing around a bottle of rum.

They glanced up when we walked in but went back to their game after waving to Charlie.

"This is where the slackers come to hide from the captain," Charlie said, a teasing tone to her voice.

The one man I didn't recognize gave a loud fake laugh and threw something small at her. "Says the biggest slacker of them all," he said.

Charlie blew him a kiss and sashayed a little before continuing to the back of the room. There was a large open crate that was filled with rum bottles.

Handing me a bottle, Charlie said, "Here. The bottles in this crate have already been diluted with water, so they last longer."

It took more effort than I'd like to admit removing the cork, but as soon as I did, I took a haul off the bottle. Sputtering, I passed Charlie the bottle.

"A bit stronger than the last drink I had," I gasped, laughing.

Charlie smirked. "Yeah, we don't add as much water as some people. Working for a captain like Kerrigan has its benefits, but it also takes a bit more rum to get through the long days and nights."

She drank from the bottle without so much as a wince.

"Want to play?" Nate asked, waving his hand over the cards.

Charlie glanced at me, and I nodded. We sat cross legged on the floor and Nate dealt the cards.

"Nora, you know Billy and Miles, right?" Nate asked.

"This is our first official meeting," Miles said. "But it's a pleasure, while also slightly terrifying."

My brow furrowed and I looked at Charlie to explain.

"Because if someone shows a little too much interest in you, Adrian might strike," she said, her hand shooting out to grab my arm. Laughing, she released me and nudged me with her elbow. "But you three won't be an issue." She turned a pointed look on the three men.

Billy and Miles held their hands up in surrender while Nate kept dealing the cards.

"You know how to play?" Charlie asked.

I bit my lip, thinking of the night I'd sat on Adrian's lap and played the game. Before I could get carried away with the memory, I nodded, and the game began. We weren't playing to win anything, just for fun.

After a few rounds of cards and passing the bottle back and forth with Charlie, I was feeling great. Laughter surrounded me as everyone teased each other and made jokes. For the first

time, I had *friends*. Not people who had to spend time with me because of my parents, or family members.

These were people I had found on my own, with a little help from Adrian, and could laugh and play games with, without feeling any pressure to behave a certain way, or censure myself.

"And a king to keep my queen company," I said, tossing down the pair I'd made. Everyone else groaned and threw their cards down, mocking outrage. I'd won four games in a row.

"Remind me not to invite you to play anymore," Nate teased.

I stuck my tongue out at him and took a swig from the rum bottle, rocking back as I did and almost falling over. Charlie caught me and we both laughed.

"You're cut off," she said. "And we should probably go get some dinner before it gets cold. Lunch was almost inedible."

"It was!" I agreed. "But yes. Dinner would be good."

Nate, Billy, and Miles joined us for dinner, sitting at the same table as us. There were only a few other people eating around us. Billy and Charlie flanked me, and they kept passing the rum bottle over me, keeping it out of my reach.

"Hey!" I laughed, grabbing for it as Billy shook it, letting the rum slosh up the sides.

"Sorry, Nora, but it's for your own good." He took a swig and leaned behind me, his arm pressing against my back as he handed it to Charlie.

Nate and Miles stiffened a second before the bottle smashed to the ground. I whipped around and Adrian gripped Billy's arm, pinning it behind his back.

"Watch yourself," Adrian growled.

"Here we go," Nate muttered.

142

Adrian's gaze flicked to Nate and his fangs glinted in the light from the lanterns.

Jumping to my feet, I fell forward over the bench and Adrian had to release Billy to catch me. He lifted me over the bench and set me back on my feet, his hands on my waist.

"Are you drunk?" he asked, his lips twitching in amusement.

I narrowed my eyes and shoved my finger into his chest. "Don't be mean to people," I slurred. "It's no wonder you don't have any friends."

"Hm." He tilted his head to the side. "You *are* drunk." Bending down, he put his arm around my legs and heaved me over his shoulder.

A squeal of surprise escaped me, and a flood of embarrassment, followed by arousal heated my entire body. Adrian carried me up the stairs, despite my protests and refusal to stay still.

"I can walk!" I cried.

Adrian kept moving, despite the comments from the crew we passed, and didn't put me down until we were in our room.

"You need to go to bed," he said, his jaw tensing as I glared at him from where he'd set me down.

I took a step toward him, our boots touching, and placed my open palm against his hard stomach. Gliding my hand up, I smirked as he stiffened, his gaze darkening.

"Will you be joining me?" I asked. "Or are you going to leave me to wake up alone again?" My smirk turned to a scowl.

143

Lifting his hand to cup my chin, his thumb stroked my jaw. "Is that why you've been avoiding me? You think I didn't want to lie in bed with you all day? Because I was tempted to."

I pursed my lips, trying not to cave to his pretty words.

"That and you started a fight with your father because the thought of marrying me is so revolting to you," I said, exaggerating a little.

Sighing, he leaned down and pressed his forehead to mine. "You don't want to marry me. Especially not on this damned ship."

I swayed with the ship, and fatigue came over me. "I made you a promise, and I'm going to keep it," I said, yawning. "And we can talk about this more tomorrow, but right now I really need to pee and then sleep."

Adrian chuckled. "I'll take you to the head. And I promise, we *will* talk more in the morning."

Once I was safely snuggled in bed, the effects of the rum brought on sleep almost instantly.

Waking in Adrian's arms was a whole new sensation I'd never known I needed in my life, but now I could never go without. I pretended to be asleep longer in the morning, just so I could stay there.

When I opened my eyes, he was already awake, and he smiled at me. He was shirtless, and I did my very best not to ogle him.

"Good morning, sweetheart," he said, kissing the top of my head. "How are you feeling?"

"I'm not sure. Ask me again once I'm out of bed." My stomach seemed okay, and my head didn't pound like I'd expected, but that could all change once I was vertical.

"I'm afraid we're going to have to get up soon. My father and Morgan will be expecting me at some point."

There was a long white scar across his right pec, beneath his tattoo of a coiled snake, that caught my attention. I traced it with my pinky until the wrappings for his wounds started. He shivered under my touch.

"What's this from?" I asked.

Gripping my hand and stopping me from continuing my trail down his torso, he lifted it to his lips and murmured, "A knife."

"Who was wielding the knife?" I pressed.

"An enemy of my father. There are quite a few of them and they all seem to think that they can use me to get to him. Little do they know I don't mean enough to him for that to work." There was no sadness in his voice, but I couldn't imagine having a father like that. One who couldn't care less about my wellbeing.

"Why do you stay?" I gazed up at him, but his eyes were staring over my head. "You could join another crew, if it's about being a pirate."

He shook his head. "Who would terrorize my father then?"

I sighed. "That's not the only reason you stay," I said. "There's got to be something else holding you here. After all he's done to you ..." I trailed off as Adrian pulled back, turning so he could sit on the edge of the bed, his back to me, and his wounds from the lashing on full display as the wrappings fell to his waist. They looked better than they should, and I wondered if he'd risked shifting to heal them faster.

Adrian ran a hand through his hair, staring at the wall. "Do you really think it would be so much better anywhere else? After everything I've done, all the people I've killed or hurt. I'd be dead without my father's flag hanging over me." His entire body stiffened, and I could tell something had shifted in him.

Sitting up, I curled my legs beneath me and leaned toward him, resting my hand on his shoulder. "I might be able to help you with that." It would be a great risk revealing my identity to him, but I trusted him. Maybe that was stupid, but I didn't care.

Adrian stood, ripping the wrappings from his waist and grabbed his tunic, pulling it on before heading to the door.

"Where are you going?" I asked.

Pausing with his hand on the doorknob, Adrian glanced back at me. "To try and convince my father to let you leave once we reach Lanteria."

I jumped off the bed. "You'll come with me, though, won't you?"

Adrian faced the door and turned the knob. "You deserve better than to be shackled to me. You'll see soon enough that I'm not a man who deserves happiness or love."

I surged forward, trying to catch his arm before he slipped out the door, shutting it between us. The outside lock slid into place, and I threw my body against the door, crying out.

"Adrian! Don't do this!" I kept banging on the door with my fists, hoping another crew member would take pity on me and let me out.

Sliding down to the floor, I wrapped my arms around my knees and clenched my eyes shut, hoping I'd open them, and this would all be a bad dream.

146

Adrian

I stood outside the door listening to Nora bang on it and yell. A few of the crew gave me weird looks but minded their own business. There was a part of me that wanted to walk back into that room and take Nora in my arms and never let her go. But I wanted to protect her more. I wanted to protect her from my father, but also from myself.

It hadn't been a lie when I said I'd be dead without my father's flag hanging over my head, and I wouldn't put Nora in harm's way by shackling her to me. There were plenty of people out there who would use her to get back at me for all I'd done, and there were even more who would kill her simply for her association with me and Kerrigan.

My mind was made up. I would convince Kerrigan to let her leave once we docked in Lanteria, even if that meant I'd have to suffer whatever punishment he deemed fit.

"She deserves better," Charlie said as she walked over from her hammock.

My hand fisted against the door, and I pushed away from it. "Which is why I'm doing this. Our betrothal was a mistake. A

lapse in my judgement. I should have never brought her into the mess that is Captain Kerrigan's world."

Charlie scoffed. "Something tells me she came willingly. Don't take away her choice in this."

Crossing my arms over my chest, I looked Charlie up and down. "What do you care?"

The stairs creaked as someone descended them. I glanced up at Polly as she approached us.

"As much as I dislike you, I like her." Charlie jerked her head at the door. "Nora is my friend, and I won't sit by and watch you treat her like this."

Polly put her hand on Charlie's shoulder. "I agree with Charlie. I don't know what's going on, but I'm on Nora's side as well. Whatever it is."

I gaped at her. Normally no one on this crew gave two shits what I did, but apparently, when it came to Nora, she had a whole host of people willing to rally behind her from only a few days spent on the ship. A laugh bubbled out of me, and I stepped aside.

"Fine. Let Nora out of her room but wait until I'm gone and don't let her follow me. If you both truly care so much about her then you'll at least agree with me that she shouldn't be subjected to spending any more time than necessary in Captain Kerrigan's presence."

"Go," Polly said, waving to the stairs. "We'll keep her occupied."

Charlie seemed like she wanted to protest, but I trusted Polly to keep her word. Leaving them behind, I headed for Kerrigan's quarters.

148

Every time I knocked on his door, I braced myself. I never knew what to expect when I walked in.

Morgan opened the door, her expression unreadable.

"I need to speak with the captain," I demanded.

"If this is about your impending nuptials, he's informed me that he only has one response for you. You will marry on this ship tonight, or else he will assume that you were lying this whole time, and he'll let Gregor have his fun with your bride to be before killing her." As always, Morgan delivered the captain's words with little emotion or inflection. It meant nothing to her, who lived or died.

Rage coursed through me. "If Gregor touches her—"

"So, you're admitting it was all a lie?" Morgan's eyebrow rose and she pursed her lips.

"Nora and I will be married tonight. Let my father know that neither he nor any of his men will lay a finger on Nora. She is *mine* and I will gut anyone who tries to take her from me." My rage won out and I loomed over Morgan, though she didn't bat an eye.

"Hm," she mused. "I'll pass it along."

If the only way I could protect Nora was to marry her, then I'd do it. I'd do whatever it took to keep her safe, even if it meant binding her to the worst monster of them all.

Nora

Charlie helped me into my dress that I was meant to wear to marry Adrian. Apparently, all his efforts to free himself of me were for naught. I hadn't seen him since he'd locked me in our room that morning.

"I feel nauseous," I told Charlie, clasping my shaking hands.

"But you look great," she joked, buttoning up the back of my dress.

I unbraided my hair and pushed it over my shoulders. The dress I wore was the same one I'd boarded the ship in. The deep purple dress was simple and nothing like what I imagined getting married in when I was younger.

"I don't envy you in the slightest," Charlie said. "I don't know what you saw in Adrian that made you want to marry him, but I have to imagine it had nothing to do with his personality." She sat down on the edge of the bed and leaned back, propping herself up with her hands.

I wanted to dispute her, but after how Adrian had locked me in our room earlier so he could try to convince his father one last time not to marry us, my heart wasn't in it.

150

Somehow Adrian had it twisted in his mind that he was saving me, or protecting me, or some other heroic bullshit. If I had guessed when I first met him, I would have said he wasn't the type. What he didn't realize was that I wasn't someone who needed protection *or* saving.

"I love him," I said as a way of explanation. It may not be true, or maybe it was. My thoughts and feelings were all jumbled. Maybe I *was* stupid. For some reason, that brought a smile to my face.

"You really do, don't you?" Charlie laughed and stood, squeezing my hand. "Well, there's no point in delaying the inevitable then."

"Land ho!" A call sounded from above us. We both looked up, as if we'd be able to see to the upper deck through the boards.

"Do you think the captain will cancel the wedding?" I asked, disappointment building in me. It wasn't that I wanted to be married, I only wanted to prove to the captain that he couldn't scare me away. And maybe I also wanted a reason for Adrian to stop going back and forth between letting himself be happy and pushing me away.

Charlie scoffed. "The captain is doing this to prove a point. He'll ensure you're married before we dock." She opened the door. Polly stood on the other side.

"Captain wants to make this quick," Polly said, holding her arm out to urge me out of the room.

"How romantic," I muttered, following Polly out of the room and up the stairs.

The sun was setting, and a sliver of land was barely visible on the horizon. Most of the crew were hanging around,

waiting for the wedding apparently, while the rest kept up with preparing the ship for making port.

A few whistles and lewd remarks were thrown my way, and I ground my jaw.

Adrian stood, back to me, facing Captain Kerrigan, who stood in front of the doors to his quarters. Morgan sat on a barrel to the captain's right, sharpening a knife. None of this was even remotely how I'd pictured my wedding day. And yet, it seemed fitting.

The first moment I had a chance at freedom, I'd fallen right into the clutches of someone who wanted to control everything around them, including me. Adrian had done his best to keep me from this, but there had never really been a choice. Kerrigan was in control, and we were pawns in his game. The only problem was, I hadn't figured out how to win yet.

Adrian turned to me when I stood in front of Captain Kerrigan and gave me a half-hearted smile that I did not return. I hadn't forgiven him yet. I'd guessed his motives for all he'd done, with help from Polly, but that didn't excuse him bouncing back and forth between wanting me and pushing me away.

"We're gathered here today," Captain Kerrigan started, diving right into the nuptials. "To bring together this man and woman in divine matrimony."

I rolled my eyes. Adrian held his hand out and I took it. We needed to keep up appearances. The reason we were marrying was because we were in love, and people in love held hands while standing at the altar. Or, in our case, in front of a captain and their crew.

My gaze kept drifting to the crew around us, sneering and whispering comments to each other. I couldn't imagine any of them actually cared to watch this show.

Adrian gripped my chin gently and brought my gaze back to him.

Eyes on me, he mouthed, his hand stroking my cheek and drifting down to take my hand that he didn't already hold.

I'd never looked into his eyes for so long. The blackness was so deep, yet it was nothing like the darkness I'd seen in his father's eyes. There was a time when my mother told me that you could always tell someone's true self by looking into their eyes.

"That's you," Adrian said.

Blinking, I realized I'd missed whatever Captain Kerrigan had said. "Oh. I do?" I glanced between the two of them, Adrian looking amused and Captain Kerrigan looking unpleasant as always.

"And do you, Adrian, take this *mermaid* shifter to be your wife?" he sneered, his disdain for me clear.

"Yes. I take *Nora* to be my wife." Adrian's small form of protest against his father by using my name made me want to laugh in Captain Kerrigan's face, but I held back.

"As captain I now pronounce you husband and wife. You may now kiss ..."

Oh gods. I'd forgotten about having to kiss Adrian in front of the entire crew. Right in front of his father, and in front of people like Gregor.

Stepping to the side, Adrian angled himself so that he was blocking me from most of the crew as he placed his hands

on either side of my face and leaned in and pressed his forehead to mine.

"Are you okay?" he whispered.

"Fine," I whispered back.

And he kissed me.

"Now everyone, back to work. We'll dock in the morning and find our prize," Captain Kerrigan shouted, everyone moving to follow his order. He turned and ducked into his quarters, Morgan slipping in behind him.

Adrian stayed in front of me, blocking my path. "Can we talk?" he asked.

Crossing my arms, I tipped my head to the side and asked, "I don't know, can we? Because this morning you seemed to want to ignore me."

He hung his head. "I know. I'm sorry I locked you in the room, it was truly for your own good."

I groaned. "Oh, enough of *that* bull shit."

His eyes widened in surprise, and he smiled.

"You think you know what's best for me. You think you can tell me what I can and can't handle. You have *no idea* what I'm capable of," I said, taking a step closer to him. "You have no idea who I really am."

"Oh?" His hand grazed up my arm. "And who are you, sweetheart?"

I shook my head. "Oh no, you don't get an answer that easily. You'll have to *work* for that. After what you've put me through, I want you to prove that you deserve to truly know me."

"And how will I go about doing that?"

I rocked back on my heels and took his hand. "Come with me."

Leading the way down the stairs to the galley, we passed crew members eating and cleaning up and went through another door and down another set of stairs to where they stored the rum. I'm sure they had other things there as well, but that was what I knew it for.

As I hoped, Charlie, Billy, and Miles were playing cards down there. Nate was missing, but I assumed he was probably helping prepare the ship for docking in the morning.

Billy and Miles looked wary when we entered the room, but Charlie smiled at me.

"The newlyweds grace us with their presence," she teased. "Come for some celebratory rum?"

I glanced up at Adrian who wore a bored expression.

"Not exactly. Mind if we join you?" I asked, holding my breath as I expected a resounding rejection.

Billy and Miles exchanged a look, but then Miles held his rum bottle out toward me and said, "You're always welcome here."

My heart swelled with joy, and I grabbed the bottle, taking a swig before passing it to Adrian. He lifted a single brow but accepted the bottle from me, drinking from it.

Sitting beside Charlie, I patted the floor and stared up at Adrian. "You going to join? Or just stand there looking like you have a stick up your ass?"

There was an intake of breath behind me and Charlie snickered. Adrian even huffed a laugh, much to my surprise.

He sat beside me and leaned in close to me, whispering in my ear, "You're out to destroy my reputation, aren't you?"

155

After a few rounds of cards, and a few rounds of the rum bottles, Adrian started to loosen up. He hadn't been entirely wrong when he'd asked if I was trying to destroy his reputation. I wanted people to see what I saw in him. If we ever separated, I wanted to leave him with people I could trust to keep him safe. There were people I could always count on when I needed them, and I wanted him to have that too. Whether he wanted it for himself or not.

Anytime someone made a joke, there was a tense moment before Adrian reacted, but that went away eventually too.

"I'll be taking that, thank you," Charlie said, taking the card Billy had discarded and throwing down the cards in her hand. "Another win for the reigning champion!"

"I take it back, I want my card back," Billy joked, reaching for the card. Charlie swatted his hand, laughing.

Leaning heavily against Adrian, I yawned, and my eyelids drooped. It was taking everything in me to stay awake.

Adrian's arm wrapped around me. "Let's get you to bed," he said softly. "Thanks for the entertainment," he said a little louder to the rest of the group.

"Anytime," Miles replied.

I couldn't remember much after that. Adrian had to carry me to bed, and I was pretty sure he left me alone in the room for a while before returning.

In the morning, I woke in his arms. Turning so I could face him, he opened his eyes and smiled at me.

"Good morning, sweetheart," he said, his voice groggy from sleep. "Have I been forgiven?"

Rolling my eyes, I said, "That's the first thing you care about when you wake up?"

"I won't be able to think about anything else until I know I've made up for my blunder. I never want you to think I don't care about you, or your feelings."

My cheeks, and other parts of me, heated.

"Almost," I said. "We've probably made port by now," I pointed out.

"Let me go see how close we are," Adrian said, extricating himself from me and the blanket. I sighed as he pulled on his trousers and tunic, and he gave me an amused look. "I'll be right back." He leaned over and kissed me.

"Fine." I stretched my arms over my head and waited for him to leave before getting out of bed.

It had been too long since my last bath, so I picked up the wash bucket in the corner. It had clean water in it, but it was cold. Taking the sponge out, I made quick work of giving myself a once over, to get rid of some of the dirt.

There was a small towel on the floor, and I grabbed that to dry myself before putting my leggings and tunic on. Sitting back on the bed, I braided my hair and decided I didn't want to wait for Adrian to return.

I peeked out my door and was surprised that no one remained belowdecks. That must mean everyone was eager to debark, even after such a short journey. Leaving the room behind, I headed to the main deck. The crew was working to prepare to dock.

John was the closest crew member who I recognized, so I went to him.

"Have we reached Lanteria?" I asked.

He gave me a wary look, most likely fearing if he talked to me that Adrian might come out of nowhere and take his eye or tongue, like he'd done to Gregor.

"Yes," he said before making himself look busy.

I took the hint and left him alone, heading for the side of the ship. We were at the docks already, where I could see swarms of people working on or near the other ships. There was a market in town beyond the docks, similar to the market in Asmara.

This wasn't my first time at the tip of Lanteria. We visited an old friend of my parents' there when I was young, but I didn't remember much from that trip.

Trying to stay out of everyone's way, I went back to my room. Adrian didn't return, but I assumed he was helping on the main deck even though I hadn't seen him when I'd been up there.

While I waited, I changed into one of the dresses I'd bought in Asmara. It was light blue with a high neck, and small white flowers embroidered along the hem of it. It was the same mid-calf length as my other one, with a tight-fitting bodice.

I could tell when we'd officially docked because a loud cheer came from the crew. It was followed by rapid footsteps on the stairs and then Adrian swung into the room, gripping the side of the doorframe, a grin on his face.

"Time to go, sweetheart," he said, out of breath. His gaze raked over me, and he held his hand out to me. "You look beautiful, as always."

Once we were off the ship, it was like the whole world opened up. I hadn't realized how truly confined I'd felt the past

few days. *Note to self: no to Thalassia, and no to spending my life on a ship.*

As if my body sensed that I was less confined, the tingling urge to shift came back. I couldn't tell if it was the mer side of me, or the lioness, which scared me. If I shifted into a lion in front of any of the crew, they'd immediately know who I was.

Adrian would know who I was. Because right now, to him, my name was Sonora. *Oh gods.* What had I done. I'd let him marry me without telling him the truth. And I'd been tempted to tell him the night before, but I'd fallen asleep before I even came close.

I glanced up at him to see if he could sense my inner panic, but he was too busy looking in shop windows as we walked down a dirt road. Sweat beaded on his forehead and the sun glistened off it.

It's fucking hot, I thought, trying to take a deep breath, but unable to. *Shit, shit, shit.* Was I having a heart attack? Or a panic attack? Did I just need to shift? What was happening?

Adrian's finger came up under my chin and he tilted my head up. "Are you okay?" he asked, concern creasing his brow.

"I think I need to shift," I said. "If we can go back to the water? I know you wanted to get food—"

"No, let's go back to the water. I know it's harder for other shifters to go so long without shifting. I've gotten used to it, but you shouldn't have to."

I nodded gratefully. I wasn't sure if it would help me, or not, but at least I was doing *something.*

As soon as I was deep enough in the water, I shifted. My muscles screamed in delight, and it was like a weight lifted off

me and I could breathe again. I'd never gone so long without shifting before. Bree and I swam together every single day back home. Mom could go longer stretches without shifting, but she had a couple hundred years of practice on us.

While I was underwater, I decided to reach out to Nix to see if she was nearby.

Nix, are you there? I couldn't sense her, but she was better than most at shielding herself and her mind.

Are you in trouble? Her voice in my mind was like getting a sliver of home back.

No. I'm fine. Better than fine but I'll explain when I see you again, I told her.

Your parents are on Jami's ship and are coming for you.

My breathing faltered and bubbles came up from my mouth. *Why? I don't want to go home yet.*

You know why. Captain Kerrigan is an old enemy of your father, and you are on his ship. Your mother is here with me. Make this easier and wait for us.

I can't do that, Nix.

I shut my mind off to her and swam as fast as I could back to shore. If my parents were on their way, we needed to leave as soon as possible. Maybe I could convince Adrian to leave the ship and his father behind.

Adrian was nowhere to be seen when I returned to the beach. I headed for the trees, thinking maybe he'd shifted too and gone to nap in a tree or something. I didn't know what snakes did.

Grabbing my dress, I pulled it over my head. I had the thought that I should check and see if anyone sold magicked

clothing in town that would shift with me, but I didn't know if we'd have time for that.

As if I'd never shifted, the tingling and nagging to shift came over me again. *Not now,* I tried to force it back down. I'd never felt such discomfort from not shifting, this was something different. Almost like the day I'd shifted into my mermaid form for the first time, but more insistent.

Unbidden, the shift came over me and I shifted into my lioness form. Thankfully the trees hid me from plain sight, but I still didn't know where Adrian was. He could appear and see me at any moment.

I decided to take a few minutes to get a feel for my lioness form and let my body calm down from the shift. It was strange to be in a whole new body. At least when I shifted into my mer form, I was still half human. In my lioness form, my senses were all heightened, and the colors had changed slightly.

I yearned to run, but I figured that would draw too much attention. Instead, I stretched and kneaded the grass with my claws. It was a similar feeling to when I dug my feet into the sand on the beach. As if something clicked inside me, I finally realized what I'd been missing all this time. *This* feeling. I could never be fully at home under the sea because I wouldn't be able to have the freedom to roam in this form.

The sun breaking through the branches hit my back and made me want to sprawl out beneath it, soaking it up. A laugh bubbled out of me, but came out as a low growl, surprising me.

A breaking branch alerted me to someone coming up behind me. On instinct, I shifted back to my human form, but, of course, my dress had been destroyed when I'd accidentally shifted before.

"What a sight for sore eyes, little lamb." Gregor's grating voice slithered over me. "Although, I guess you're not such a little lamb after all."

I wrapped my arms around myself, trying to hide as much of my body as possible.

Gregor stood between two trees back toward the beach with Lyle directly behind him.

"Captain will be so thrilled to know that his prize has been right under his nose this whole time," Gregor sneered. "And the reward we'll get for bringing you to him."

As if she was one of the gods herself, Marley dropped from the sky, or the tree more likely, and shoved a dagger into each of the backs of Gregor and Lyle's skulls. They both dropped to the ground, dead.

I stood, stunned, for a moment before she ran to me and threw a cloak over my shoulders, wrapping an arm around me.

"You're lucky I stole this from your Aunt Lia a few years back and kept it on me in case I went anywhere colder than Asmara," she said.

I tugged the edges of the cloak close. "Thank you," I mumbled, still in shock.

"Come on. Let's go get you some real clothes."

Marley found me a new dress, almost identical to the one I'd ruined, and we stopped at a bakery for food.

"I talked with Nix while I was in the water," I said, picking at my muffin.

Marley pursed her lips and nodded. "I tried to keep them at bay. I'm sorry, I know things were going well for you and Adrian."

162

I laughed. "As if you could keep *my dad* at bay. I do appreciate your trying."

Marley usually wasn't the affectionate type, so I was surprised when she reached across the table and put her hand over mine.

"Your identity is still a secret on the ship, since I took care of you know who," she said. "If you want to stay with Adrian for a little while longer, I won't stop you."

"But you'll keep following me?" I asked, almost hopeful, because I didn't think I could do this without her.

"Of course. Unless your dad finds out about this and kills me. He's been looking for an excuse for years." She scrunched her nose and leaned back, removing her hand from mine. "And I can't promise Nix and your mother won't do something crazy, but I don't think they'd risk revealing your identity like that."

"I want to stay," I said quietly, worrying if I said it too loud my family would suddenly surround me and force me to go home.

"So, stay," she said.

"You didn't happen to see where Adrian went earlier? He was supposed to wait for me on the beach, but when I came out of the water he'd gone." I was trying not to worry about him, but it was hard to think he wouldn't come looking for me.

Marley nodded. "Morgan came and got him. He did look a bit hesitant to leave, if that makes you feel better."

That *didn't* make me feel any better. Morgan must have been fetching him for Captain Kerrigan.

Leaving the bakery, I went out the front door and Marley out the back at separate times to be sure no one would see us together.

I kept my eye out for any of the crew as I made my way back to the ship, but I didn't see anyone I recognized. No one should miss Gregor or Lyle right away, so at least I would have a chance to talk with Adrian and find a way to explain their absence.

There were a few crew members on the main deck when I boarded the ship, but none I knew well enough to talk to.

"Welcome back, Nora." Captain Kerrigan stood in the doorway to his quarters looking too smug for my liking. "Come in, please."

I did a quick scan of my surroundings, but Adrian wasn't around. I had a good feeling he was already in the captain's quarters, so I moved forward to meet my fate.

Morgan stood beside Captain Kerrigan's desk as intimidating as ever.

"Nice of you to join us, Leonora," she said, her tone monotone.

"What is this?" I asked, turning back to Captain Kerrigan as he shut the door between us and freedom.

"So, you don't deny it?"

I whipped around when I heard Adrian's voice, relief washing over me until I realized what he was asking.

So, you don't deny it?

Deny it ... Oh gods. Morgan had called me by my real name. They knew. I backed away on instinct, but Captain Kerrigan came up behind me, blocking my path.

164

"Oh, how the gods have blessed me, dropping you *right* into my lap." Captain Kerrigan gripped my upper arms, holding me in place. "Well, I guess Adrian's lap is more accurate." He chuckled darkly.

There was only one way out of this, so I looked at Adrian. "Adrian, please, I didn't mean for this to happen. I wanted to tell you the truth, but I wasn't sure—"

"You said you trusted me, but that was a lie." His gaze was hard and gave away nothing. I had no idea whether he was acting or *truly* upset with me.

"No! I do trust you!" I struggled to break free of Captain Kerrigan's hold. I could shift, but then I would become a threat, and they might kill me.

"Then tell me why you used me to get close to my father?" Adrian stayed beside Captain Kerrigan's desk, almost as if he was afraid to approach me.

The laugh that escaped me was almost manic. Did he truly believe such a thing?

"Don't laugh. I *saw* you with that red head. One of Captain Finn's old crew members. And I thought I heard you talking to someone when I left you alone in the inn back in Asmara, but I gave you the benefit of the doubt. Now I realize I was wrong to do that."

Captain Kerrigan dipped his chin so his mouth was right beside my ear. "Your father's people have been following us so you can all figure out my secrets and take me down, isn't that right?" His hot breath against my cheek made me squirm in his grip. "You just didn't take into account that you'd be caught before you could finish your plan, and now you're *mine.*"

165

Craning my neck to try and get his face away from me, I refocused on Adrian.

"You're not going to believe me, no matter what I say. I *am* Leonora. I am Finn and Viv's daughter. But I couldn't give two shits about your father or this stupid ship. I'm here for *you*. Why the fuck else would I come back here?"

"Ugh," Captain Kerrigan groaned, pushing me away from him. "Tie her up, Morgan. And put her in the brig."

I planned to shift into my lioness form once I was alone with Morgan, but when she approached me, she pulled out a needle and stabbed my arm with it.

"Shit! What was that?" I gasped, rubbing the spot.

"Shifter suppressant," Morgan stated.

"What?" I'd never heard of such a thing, but I could feel it taking effect. It moved through my veins like fire, burning away the ability to use *any* of my magic. Out of pure panic, I tried to extend my claws, mermaid or lion it didn't matter, neither appeared.

Fatigue washed over me, and I became lightheaded. Morgan kicked the backs of my legs, making me drop to the floor, my knees cracking against the wood. I hissed in pain. She tied my hands together behind my back, not even trying to be gentle, not that I'd expected that from her.

I refused to look at Adrian as he watched.

Marley was going to be pissed she'd let me come back on the ship for me to be captured.

"My parents were right. I should have stayed away from pirates," I said to no one in particular. That was one of the worst things to come out of this. *My parents were right.* They would never trust me to go off on my own again, and I couldn't blame

166

them. I'd ended up in the exact situation they'd warned me about. Someone who had a vendetta against my dad *and* wanted to sell me to some mage or healer to experiment on.

In one last ditch effort to try and get through to Adrian, while Morgan yanked me to my feet and pushed me toward the door, I caught his eye.

"I still don't regret staying," I said. I thought I caught a flicker of some emotion other than his usual unreadable mask, but it was there and gone too quickly to be sure I hadn't imagined it.

"Wait," Captain Kerrigan said. "Here." He draped a cloak over my shoulders to hide the ropes tying my hands behind my back. "In case they're watching. And, Nora, act normal please. I may not be able to kill you, but I have more creative ways to make you suffer."

Morgan put her arm around my shoulders, as if leading me out of the room like a friend rather than a captor. We'd left port and the sun had set since I'd been in the captain's quarters and we were already too far from land to be able to swim back without being able to shift, especially with my hands tied. They must have been prepared to shove off the moment I stepped foot back onto the ship. It was almost like the entire crew was in on my capture.

Stupid, stupid.

Adrian had been right. I was stupid. Stupid to think I could hide in plain sight, and stupid to think I could have an adventure ending in a love story like my parents had.

The brig was two flights down, right below the crew's quarters. I was glad to be the only prisoner since it was a small space, barely big enough for one. Once Morgan left I sat down,

my hands still tied behind me, and leaned my head against the wall.

"Marley," I spoke normally, not trying to call attention to myself, but hoping she'd be close by. "If you can hear me, Nix was right. I should have gone home."

As if I'd summoned her, she flew in through a porthole and shifted before my eyes.

"I'm getting you out of here," she said, fiddling with the lock and a pick.

"No. There's no point. I can't shift if I escape. They used some kind of shifter suppressant on me. I didn't even know there *was* such a thing."

"I've heard of it, but I didn't realize people had access to it. I thought it was only available in prisons, or for emergencies in the castles." She didn't stop trying to pick the lock. "You can swim long enough for Nix and your mother to arrive, and then they can swim you back to Jami's ship."

"Before I'm spotted by one of Captain Kerrigan's men?" I sighed and shook my head. "It's a bad plan. Wait to let me out until they're here."

The floorboards above us creaked and footsteps moved toward the stairs.

"Go!" I hissed. "You won't be saving anyone if you get captured too!"

She scoffed. "As if I'd let them catch me." She stepped away from the lock, though. "I'll be back for you. I won't go far."

Whoever was coming down the stairs stopped halfway. I could see black boots, and I held my breath when I recognized

the black trousers. Every other crew member wore tan or brown trousers.

"Too scared to face me and own up to your mistakes?" I said, my anger seeping out in my tone. I wasn't going to let him look down on me, so I stood up, which was made slightly difficult by the fact that my hands were still tied behind my back.

Slowly, Adrian came down the rest of the stairs, his face blank and his posture relaxed. I lifted my chin and stared him down. I wouldn't show him fear.

"You lied to me," he stated.

"Only once. And it was only a half lie. People *do* call me Nora." I shrugged, trying to play at nonchalance like he did. "And technically, I lied to your father, not you. *You* never asked my name."

He licked his lips as he approached my prison, and I silently cursed myself that I was still so attracted to him.

"You know," I started, biting my bottom lip. "You aren't who I thought you were either. I didn't take you for someone who would so easily be swayed by Daddy's stories of secret plots. Especially when you yourself have your own plot against him."

His nostrils flared, the only indication I'd struck the truth.

I laughed. "I knew it! You want to prove to him that you're a better pirate, a *crueler* pirate."

Adrian strolled the last few steps to the bars separating us and looked me over before reaching out and gripping my chin with his thumb and forefinger. There was nowhere for me to go, so I didn't bother trying to pull away.

"You're right, sweetheart."

169

One second, he was standing on the opposite side of the bars, and then he shifted into a snake and shifted back inside the brig with me. His fangs snapped out and he put a hand around my throat, gripping lightly, but holding me in place. He ran his nose up the length of my neck until his mouth was beside my ear.

"Do you still trust me?" he asked, sending chills through my whole body while simultaneously starting a fire in my core.

"Yes," I breathed.

"Good girl." He removed his hand from my throat, dragging his fangs along it and kissed the space between my neck and shoulders.

I pressed myself against him but couldn't move my arms because they were still tied.

"This isn't fair," I gasped. "I can't touch you."

A laugh rumbled through him, but he pulled out a dagger and cut the ropes for me. Before I could wrap my arms around him like I wanted to, he grabbed my wrists and pinned my arms above my head with one hand.

"Hey," I huffed.

His lips covered mine, and his tongue swept into my mouth. I ground against him, moaning as his hard length rubbed against my core.

The stairs creaked and in a matter of seconds, Adrian was back outside of the bars, leaving me hot and breathless. He winked and backed away from me. I tried my best to return my breathing to normal and not look like we'd just done what we'd done.

Placing my hands behind my back, I pretended they were still tied.

"I said you could have five minutes," Morgan said as she came down the stairs. She looked between the two of us, eyes narrowed as if she knew exactly what had almost happened. "No one can find Gregor or Lyle, you haven't seen them, have you?"

Adrian frowned. "Are you accusing me of something?"

"You cut out Lyle's tongue for talking shit about Polly two years ago, and you carved out Gregor's eye just the other night. So, sorry for thinking you may have made them disappear." Morgan said all this with a simple raised brow. The way she always seemed so unbothered by everyone's shit made me realize how Adrian had learned to hold his mask so well. She was constantly putting on an act just like he was.

"I haven't seen them. I'll be up in one minute, if I'm a second longer, you can throw me overboard, I know you've been tempted to try that one on me for a while."

Morgan rolled her eyes and went back up the stairs.

"You won't find Gregor or Lyle," I said when I was sure she was gone.

Adrian came back over to the bars but didn't come inside again.

"What did you do to them, sweetheart?" He smirked as if imagining me killing those men brought him joy.

"I did nothing. Marley killed them. They saw me shift into a lioness, and of course when I shifted back my dress was destroyed and there they were."

Fire blazed in his eyes, and he scowled. "They deserved to die for that alone." His expression changed and realization widened his eyes. "Lioness?"

"I won't lie to you anymore, Adrian. Your father was right and I'm the world's first dual shifter. I didn't know for sure until that night your father attacked me outside the bar."

"I'm throwing you overboard!" Morgan called down the stairs.

"I'm walking up the stairs," Adrian called back. Instead, he pulled a key from his pocket and unlocked my cage, opening the door.

"You had that the whole time?" I whisper-yelled.

Marley came soaring back through the port hole, shifting and landing right beside me. She held a dagger up to Adrian. His eyes widened in surprise, and he lifted both of his hands in surrender.

"I'll take it from here," she growled.

I put a hand on her arm, trying to get her to lower the dagger. "Marley, it's okay. He's the one who let me out."

"Oh, I know who he is and what he's done."

Steps on the stairs warned us that Morgan was returning.

"I'll take care of her, you get Nora out of here," Adrian said, running over to the stairs. "I told you I was coming," he told Morgan, meeting her halfway before she'd see me and Marley.

"And it was well over a minute, so I'm throwing you overboard," Morgan said matter-of-factly.

Their footsteps receded and once it was quiet, we moved toward the stairs.

"Your mother and Nix are waiting for you. They're also pissed at me, so if you could put in a good word for me, it would be much appreciated," Marley said.

I shook my head, of course she was worried about that *now*. "Let's get off this ship first, and then we'll worry about that."

We considered going out the porthole, but it was slightly too small for me to fit through. So, we took the stairs.

At the top of the stairs, we realized we were not getting out without being seen. There were already some crew members in their hammocks, and not all of them were asleep.

Marley poked her head over the opening to the steps to see if there was a path we could take that would avoid most people.

"I think our best option is to act normal and just go. We'll fight our way out if we have to." She grabbed a dagger from a sheath in her boot and handed it to me.

"I should have weapons that can shift with me," I whispered. "For future times like this."

"Talk to your dad." She gripped her own dagger in her hand.

Standing as casually as possible, she began her walk across the room. I waited a few seconds and then followed. At first, we got a few glances but not much else, but then someone realized Marley didn't belong.

"Oy!" someone shouted, and Marley waved to me to run, so I did. She lagged, taking out the pirate closest to us. I kept moving toward the next set of stairs. I'd made it halfway up them with Marley close behind when a gunshot ran out and I screamed in agony as the bullet tore through my leg.

"Nora!" Marley cried.

"Don't shoot, you idiot!" someone yelled. "The captain wants them alive."

173

I tried to move, but the pain kept me on my ass. More pirates were closing in on us and Marley wasn't about to leave me there alone. We'd failed.

Adrian

Morgan talked my father into letting her make me walk the plank. I'd be fished out of the water after, but she'd be satisfied that I'd paid my price for defying her. So, a few of the crew members were preparing the plank.

I was convinced she was only doing it to make herself laugh. Not that I'd ever seen her laugh, but if she did, this would be what would bring it about.

Morgan, Kerrigan, and I stood in front of the door to Kerrigan's quarters, watching the crew work.

"Now that we have Leonora, Finn won't be far behind. I can finally exact my revenge and once he's dead, there will be no one to stop me from selling the girl to the highest bidder." My father spoke as if he'd already won. Little did he know, I'd foiled his plans once again. Nora would be off the ship in a matter of minutes, and she'd be free to live her life far from my father or myself.

I'd truly doubted her for a minute, and I'd regret that for the rest of my life. She deserved far better than me, but I'd had

to taste her one last time before I let her go. I'd never be free of the memory of her.

A gunshot made my heart skip a beat.

Nora. Without considering keeping up appearances, I ran to the stairs leading to the crew's quarters and froze when Nora looked up at me from where she'd crumpled halfway up the stairs, blood coating her hands.

It was as if I was frozen in time, staring down at Nora. Marley was at the foot of the stairs, fighting with one of the crew.

"Well, this is an interesting turn of events," Kerrigan said from behind me. He stood looking over my shoulder at the scene below us.

"What would you like me to do?" I asked, doing my best to pretend it wasn't gutting me not to go to Nora. But if I wanted to get her out of this alive, I needed to play it right.

"Morgan, fetch Marley. I'd like to have a chat with her," Kerrigan commanded. "And you." He squeezed my shoulder to the point of pain. "Get the girl and put something on her wound so she doesn't bleed out. I need her *alive.*"

I nodded and did as he said. When I reached Nora, I crouched down, putting one arm beneath her knees and one at her back, lifting her smoothly. She cried out in pain, but I didn't flinch. My father needed to believe I had nothing to do with her escape and that Marley had let her out. Otherwise, this would never work.

Marley had surrendered herself to Morgan, giving up her dagger. She locked eyes with me and mouthed, *get her out.* I gave her no indication I'd understood in case Kerrigan's eyes were on me.

176

"I've got you," I told Nora, turning to take her up the stairs.

My mind was reeling as I formulated a plan. I had seconds to enact it if I wanted to get Nora off this ship. Gripping Nora tighter, I moved in the direction of the plank.

Billy and Miles were on either side of the plank, and Billy jerked his head toward it.

"My quarters," Kerrigan snapped.

That's when I ran and jumped onto the plank running straight off the end. Nora screamed as we fell, and we hit the water with a slap.

The sea dragged us down and I couldn't see anything. Nora clung to me, and I to her. At first, I wondered if we'd drown. The shifter suppressant wouldn't wear off on her for another few hours. But then, a hand gripped my arm, and Nora was torn from me, and we were rising.

As soon as I broke through the surface, dark rage-filled eyes stared into mine.

"Where is she?" the woman hissed.

"She was taken from me underwater," I explained. "I assumed it was one of you."

"Not Nora! Marley, you idiot!" she yelled even though I was only inches away.

"She told me to get Nora out, so I did!" I yelled back. We were still too close to the ship for comfort, and I wished we'd get moving.

"Nix! Leave him alone!" Hearing Nora's voice took a weight off my chest, and I turned to see her with her arm over another mermaid's shoulders. This mermaid had golden eyes

and close-cropped brown hair, left long on top to swoop over her forehead.

From the family resemblance, I could guess she was Nora's mother, Viv.

"We need to go," Viv said. "Marley can handle herself, and Kerrigan won't hurt her if he truly wants Finn to come to him."

"Fine," Nix snapped.

"Nora needs help before we go anywhere," I said.

Viv dove beneath the surface and I moved over to Nora, helping to keep her afloat.

"Mom can heal my leg enough so it will stop bleeding," Nora explained, her voice strained. It was too dark to see anything outside of where we drifted. The moon was only half full that night, and the ship had moved further away, taking any light it had provided with it.

Nora's eyes clenched shut and she let out a long breath.

"It's alright, I've got you," I said, though my legs were already getting tired from supporting us both. I figured Nix could much more easily help Nora, but I didn't want to let her go.

Viv resurfaced and took hold of Nora again.

"Okay, let's go," she said. "Nix, you take Adrian."

Nix swam over to me and grabbed my arms, turning so they were draped over her shoulders and started swimming. Viv and Nora were right behind us.

"I'm sorry, Mom," Nora said.

If Viv responded, I didn't hear it.

We were in the water for over an hour before we came to another ship. The mermaids moved much faster than I could have swum, even in my snake form.

A rope was lowered for us, and we sent Nora up first. She clung to the rope while she was pulled up, and then it was lowered for each of us in turn. I worried that when it came to me, they wouldn't bother reeling me in, but they did.

I almost wished they hadn't when I stood on the deck and every single person stared at me with looks of disdain. Nora was gone, probably taken to be tended to since she'd been shot, but I wished I'd had her by my side. It was the first time in my life since my mother abandoned me that I had the feeling I needed someone else.

"You're Kerrigan's son?" The man who spoke was definitely Nora's father, Captain Finn. They had the same eyes.

"Yes, sir— Er, Captain," I corrected, unsure how to address him.

"Jami's the captain of this ship. I haven't held that title in a long time," Finn corrected me.

"Right." I cleared my throat. "Is Nora—"

"Nora is no longer your concern," Finn said, stepping forward and looking me up and down.

A woman with bright green hair and violet eyes pushed past Finn and another man, who I assumed was Jami, the captain. "Don't scare the poor boy, Finn," she said, smiling at me.

"I don't scare easily," I said, putting on my mask of indifference. I wasn't going to let these people intimidate me. I'd grown up with *Kerrigan* for a father, for the gods' sakes.

Finn's lip curled, but the woman skipped forward and held her hand out to me.

"I'm Nora's Aunt Lia, it's a pleasure to meet you," she said.

I took her hand with a smirk and kissed it. "The pleasure is mine."

"Don't drool, Lia, it's unbecoming," Nix said. She'd reappeared without me noticing. "He's the reason Marley is stuck back on Kerrigan's ship."

Lia sighed and stepped back. "Would you like me to go with you to fetch her?" she asked, as if it would be so easy.

"No!" Jami snapped. "We'll find a better, safer way to get Marley back. Besides, she's probably having the time of her life messing with Kerrigan."

Lia sauntered over to Jami and put her hand on his chest. "So, bossy. I like it. Let's go." She tugged the lapel of his jacket and pulled him away from the rest of the group.

Finn dragged his hand down his face while the rest of the crew dispersed.

I cocked my eyebrow. "So, you're the man my father wants dead," I said.

"And you're the man *I* want dead," Finn sneered.

"What a conundrum," I deadpanned.

Nix came back, handing a pair of shackles to Finn. "Here," she said.

I didn't bother trying to run. There was no point. I could shift and escape into the water easily enough, but I wasn't going to leave Nora behind, and if I returned to Kerrigan's ship, I'd meet a worse fate. So, I put my wrists out and tilted my head.

"Do it, then," I said.

Finn and I stared each other down for what felt like an eternity until Nix took the shackles back and slapped them on my wrists. I held them out in front of me, letting the short chain dangle between the shackles.

"Until he can be proven to be trustworthy," Nix said, almost like she needed to convince Finn.

If Finn had slapped the shackles on me himself, I wouldn't have blamed him. I was the son of his greatest enemy. He had a right to be suspicious of me.

The door to the captain's quarters creaked open and Viv slipped out. "Can you take a break from the stare down for a few minutes? Nora wants to see you," she said to Finn.

I'd been hoping Nora would ask for me first, but I'd have to suffer the awkwardness of dealing with her family a little while longer. They may not even *let* me see her.

"Take him to the brig, Nix," Finn said before disappearing into the captain's quarters.

"I've got him, Nix," Viv said. Nix narrowed her eyes, but turned on her heel and strode away, leaving us alone. "Let's take a walk." Viv waved to me to join her as she headed for the stairs leading up to the helm. She glanced pointedly at the shackles on my wrists and lifted her brow. "They didn't shackle your ankles. You can still walk, can't you?"

Her snarky question reminded me of something Nora would say, and I couldn't help smirking. I walked beside her.

"Nora filled me in on a lot." Viv glanced over at me. "But I want to hear from you."

"What would you like to know?" I asked.

181

"Your father wanted to find and capture Nora; do you know why?" From the way she asked, I could tell she knew the answer and was only trying to feel out if *I* knew.

Marley had seen Nora shift into a lioness, so even if Nora hadn't told her mother about that, she knew.

"I do. She's both a mermaid and a lion shifter," I said, not skirting around what she wanted to hear. "A dual shifter."

"The first to ever exist," Viv confirmed.

I nodded. "He didn't know when he first had her join us on the ship. *I* didn't even know."

We stopped at the back of the boat and Viv leaned against it, crossing her arms over her chest.

"Humer started this mess with me, over forty years ago." She laughed, but I wasn't sure what she was talking about, or why it was funny. "And I'd prayed to all the gods that it would end with me. Until this week, I still thought it might have, and that this hunt was all for nothing."

"But Nora shifted into a lioness," I said, and Viv sighed. "So now what?"

"Now she'll need to be kept safe and away from anyone who wants to use her to create more dual shifters. People like your father, who wants to sell her to someone who would experiment on her like Humer did to me and so many others."

There was a haunted look in her eyes, and I couldn't even begin to imagine what it must have been like for her. The thought of anyone trying to do that to Nora set my teeth on edge and lit a fire in my veins.

"I'd like to see them try," I ground out.

Viv patted my arm. "They will. Thankfully she has a whole host of people who are willing to do anything to protect her, for which I'm eternally grateful."

"She's very lucky." I had no one who would do that for me. If mine and Nora's roles were reversed, I'd have a line of people ready to sell me off. Shit, my father would have sold me the day my mother left me on his ship if he hadn't had a use for my venom.

Nodding slowly, Viv said, "She is. But what I need to know is, if you're to stay, are you willing to see this through? To make sure she stays out of harm's way and out of a cage?"

I thought of the cage I'd practically helped put her in only a few hours ago. I'd kill anyone who so much as looked at Nora the wrong way, but would I be what she truly needed, and wanted at the end of the day?

"If Nora will have me."

"Good answer." Viv smirked. "She did ask for you before Finn, you know."

"Yeah?" That would have made me laugh, but I figured I shouldn't gloat in front of Viv.

"But Finn would have killed you right then and there if he'd heard that." Amusement sparked in her gaze.

I dipped my head to her. "Thank you for sparing me, then. I hope I can someday repay the kindness."

"Oh, don't worry, I'll think of something. And I hope you'll understand why we can't let you see Nora just yet." Her eyes flicked to my shackles.

I strained against them for the first time since they'd been put on, anger and disbelief coursing through me.

"What do you think I'll do to her?" I asked, trying to keep my voice calm.

"Mom!" A younger, feminine voice rang out, tearing Viv's attention from me. "Can I— Oh." A younger version of Nora appeared at the top of the stairs; except she had Viv's golden eyes, while Nora had her father's storm-gray eyes. "I didn't realize you were busy." She blushed and dipped her head to her mother.

"It's alright, Bree. This is Nora's new friend, Adrian." She waved her hand toward me.

I inclined my head to Bree. "It's nice to meet you, Bree."

"You too." She flicked her gaze back to her mother. "Can I go with Nix to see if we can spy on Captain Kerrigan and find out if Marley's okay?"

Viv stiffened. "Excuse me," she said to me. "Let's talk about this." She took Bree's hand and led her back down the stairs.

Almost as if from thin air, Nix appeared at my side.

"Let's go." She took my arm, and I let her lead me down to the brig. It was almost identical to the one of Kerrigan's ship. "Enjoy your stay," Nix said before slipping back up the stairs. She moved silently, which was impressive.

Sitting on the floor and resting my forearms on my knees, I let my shackles dangle out before me.

Being on this ship felt like a whole other world than the *Wave Breaker*. I didn't know what to think or how to act. Should I be watching my back, or trying to make allies? Was this all a trap and they were going to try to use me against my

father as had happened so many times in the past? The shackles clanked as I twisted my wrists.

Minutes or hours passed while I watched the sky through a small porthole, I couldn't be sure. But Finn found me and pulled up a chair outside of the brig, not saying anything for a while.

"I don't trust you," he finally said.

I lifted my hands, the shackles scraping my wrists and grunted, "Clearly."

"But Nora does. And she has requested that I give you a chance to prove yourself."

I almost scoffed but thought better of it. *Prove myself.* I'd been fighting to prove myself my whole life and it had yet to lead to any sort of reward. My father couldn't stand me, I disappointed Morgan time and again, and everyone else I knew hated me.

"What would that entail?" I asked.

"To start, help me get Marley back from your father. I assume he will use her as leverage to get to me now that he no longer has Nora to bargain with."

"I betrayed my father by taking Nora off that ship, he'll kill me on sight." There was no doubt in mind about that. He had enough of my venom stored up so that he could find a new snake shifter to take my place before he needed more.

"So, is that a no?" Finn's brow rose.

I'd told Nora that I'd be dead without my father's flag hanging above my head, so what would happen if he were gone? If I helped these people go after him and take him down, where would that leave me? There was no way my father would ever let

me back on his ship, so whatever happened, it didn't matter anymore. I'd help them to protect Nora.

"We're going to need a good plan," I said. "But I want to see Nora first." Lifting my wrists, I added, "Without these. She doesn't need to know about these."

Finn pursed his lips, and his jaw moved from side to side. "Tell me about yourself, Adrian."

"Excuse me?" I asked, incredulously.

"You heard me. Why should I let you see my daughter? What makes you *worthy* of her time?" Finn looked down his nose at me.

"I'm the son of Kerrigan and Elise, raised to be as ruthless as my father, and all too happy to hurt anyone who has wronged me. I'm *not* worthy of Nora. But for some reason, that hasn't stopped her from wanting me around." I decided to stick with brutal honesty, because Finn didn't seem like a man who would care for anything less.

Leaning forward, resting his forearms on his thighs and clasping his hands out in front of him, Finn looked me up and down. "You know who I am. Through stories, or from your father." He paused, clearly waiting for an answer.

"I do," I supplied.

"Then you know what I'm capable of if you so much as *think* about hurting my daughter."

"I would never."

Finn shook his head. "I'm assuming Viv went easy on you, because despite what she's been through, she still has the ability to see the goodness in people. That doesn't mean that she won't be the one driving a dagger through your heart if you cross our family."

186

I kept my face neutral. This was all an intimidation tactic, which I was all too used to from dealing with my own father. "As I said, I would never hurt Nora. I'd give my life to keep her safe every time."

Continuing, Finn said, "Because my daughter trusts you, and I trust her judgement, I'll give the two of you a few minutes to talk. Then, you'll stay away from her until I decide if *I* trust you or not."

I blinked in surprise. Apparently, I'd said something right. Or maybe Finn was taking pity on me and allowing me one last chance to talk with Nora before he'd throw me overboard. That seemed the more likely scenario, but I'd take it if it meant seeing Nora again.

Nora

Jami's bed was comfortable, but I felt bad that my parents had commandeered it for me. It wasn't like I needed it. The worst of my wounds had been healed by my mom, and now it was only sore.

Viv, Bree, and Nix were arguing in the office of Jami's quarters, and though I could hear the entire conversation, I didn't chime in. Nix wanted to try and check up on Marley, and Bree wanted to go with her, but Viv was against either of them going anywhere.

Marley was only in that situation because of me. I could have made everyone's lives easier and just gone with Nix back in Lanteria. None of this would have happened and Marley would be safe with us. I couldn't even imagine what Nix must be feeling, to have the woman she loved being held by one of the most feared pirates.

Guilt clenched my stomach. *Probably similar to knowing your daughter was on a ship with one of the most feared pirates who wanted to sell her off to be experimented on.*

Yeah. Probably a little like that. And I'd willingly put myself in that situation. I was selfish. This whole excursion had been selfish. I should have stayed home and—

The arguing ceased.

"Pardon my interruption."

Adrian. Ah yes. My motivation for being so selfish.

I bit my lip and balled the blanket beneath me up in my fists.

"Nora's through there," Bree said. I could hear the excitement in her voice. Like me, she'd been sheltered, and this was the most exciting thing she'd ever been involved with. Sure, it was dangerous excitement, but it was better than nothing.

"Let's give them a minute alone," Viv said, and the door clicked shut.

Silence followed, and all I heard were Adrian's steps as he came around the wall separating the bedroom from the office. There was no door, so we wouldn't have much privacy, but I didn't care about that. I just needed to see him.

He stopped when he saw me, his indifferent mask firmly in place.

"You look better," he said, his voice stiff.

Shifting to sit up a little taller, I winced and said, "A little sore, but nothing too serious."

"You were shot," he stated matter-of-factly, as if I weren't aware.

"I was." I unballed my fists and smoothed out the blankets.

Adrian watched my movements. "Hm."

"Are you going to stand over there the whole time? Do you need me to come to you?" I teased.

189

He gave the barest hint of a smile before it disappeared, and he cleared his throat, his mask donned once more.

"You're going to make this hard on me, aren't you?" I swung my legs over the side of the bed and stood. I still wore the dress Marley had bought for me, though it had blood stains on it. My mom had promised to get me something else to wear, but clearly, she'd been distracted.

Adrian's gaze flicked to those blood stains and his jaw ticked.

Each step toward him I took, it seemed like he became even more tightly wound. His fists clenched at his sides and his entire body was rigid. It reminded me of a snake preparing to strike, and I wanted to see how far I had to push him to make him snap.

"Nora," he warned.

I stood toe to toe with him. My bare feet looked so small compared to his heavy, black boots. Going up on my tiptoes, I trailed my fingers up his arms before cupping his face in my hands. He didn't fight me as I pulled his lips down to mine and kissed him lightly.

"You don't need to wear your mask here. I've already seen what's on the other side," I said quietly.

Pressing his forehead to mine, he gently grabbed my wrists and lowered my hands to my sides. "It's not as easy as that. It's not a mask anymore, it's just who I am."

"Fine. Then I'll love this side of you too," I said.

It wasn't until I saw the surprise on Adrian's face that I realized what had come out of my mouth.

"I mean ... I didn't mean ... If you don't," I scrambled, pulling away.

He put a finger to my lips. "Let me have this for a minute before you take it back." He closed his eyes for a few seconds, breathing deeply.

I gave him an incredulous look. "I'm not taking it back. I didn't mean for it to come out that way, but that doesn't mean it's not what I feel."

"Please don't play with me, Nora. There's no possible way you could love me."

"Well, I do! And I'm not taking it back, so you're stuck with it." I stuck my tongue out and skipped backward.

One step and he was back in reach of me, snatching my hand and pulling me back against him. "Love shouldn't be given so freely to men like me, Nora," he said, his mouth beside my ear.

A thrill ran up my spine.

"No?" I gasped, my breathing becoming labored as desire coiled low in my core.

He placed his hand flat over my stomach and slowly, *too* slowly, it crept down, bunching up my dress as he went.

"No one has ever loved me, Nora. It's not possible."

It clicked. This wasn't about *me*. Turning in his arms, I faced him and put my hands at the back of his neck, playing with the ends of his hair.

"It *is* possible," I said. "Because I love you. I love you even if you don't love me. I love you because of who you are, and what you've done. The good and the bad."

"You think I don't love you?" He gripped my thigh and hitched my leg up on his hip. "Nora, *I can't think straight with you around.* Any time you walk in a room, I can't breathe, and the thought of ever living a life without you *terrifies* me."

191

My breathing hitched and I fluttered my lashes. "So?" I pressed. Waiting for him to say the three words he claimed to feel.

His hand trailed down my thigh, which was still hitched up, toward my slick core. When he reached my center, his brows rose in surprise.

"The dress was our only purchase earlier," I said, smirking. "Undergarments weren't exactly a priority."

Without warning, he pumped two fingers inside me, making me gasp.

"What a shame," he said.

As he moved his fingers inside me, I leaned my head back and moaned. "Gods, Adrian."

He moved faster, toying with my clit with his thumb. His mouth captured mine to stifle my moans so we wouldn't be overheard, and when I finished on his hand, I slumped against him, and he lowered my leg, so I was standing on my own two feet.

"Did I mention I love you?" I said, my forehead against his chest as I tried to catch my breath.

"Mm," he hummed, the sound vibrating through me. "We'll see how long that lasts."

"I hate you," I huffed and laughed.

"I'll admit, that didn't last as long as I thought it would." He tipped my chin up with his forefinger.

"But I still love you." I smirked. "You're not scaring me off that easily."

Someone knocked on the door and I jumped away from Adrian. He barely blinked.

The evidence of what we'd done was still between my thighs and on his hand. At least my dress hid half of that issue.

I motioned to him frantically and he laughed before sticking his fingers into his mouth and pulling them out tauntingly slow.

That alone had me hot all over again.

"Come in!" I called, moving to the doorway between the office and bedroom so I could see who came in.

Lia poked her head in with her hand over her eyes and said, "I'm just letting you know that food is ready and going fast if you're hungry."

"We're decent, Aunt Lia, you don't need to cover your eyes," I said.

She laughed and dropped her hand. "Can't be too safe. Oh!" Pushing the door fully open, she came in, holding a pile of clothes out to me. "You probably want these."

I met her halfway and took them. Adrian stepped into the doorway behind me and leaned his shoulder against the wall, crossing his arms.

"We'll have a chat soon, Adrian," Lia said, giving him a once over. "I know Viv went too easy on you."

I groaned. "Please don't," I said. "Mom and Dad have already talked with him, isn't that enough?"

Lia scoffed. "Never. Once Nix calms down enough not to try and strangle him when she sees him, she'll probably have a go as well. So, don't get comfortable just yet."

Once she'd left, I turned to Adrian.

"I am so sorry and will understand if you decide to jump ship and swim the rest of the way to Asmara."

"You'd let someone you *love* go so easily?" he teased, putting his hands on my waist and tracing circles with his thumbs.

"Oh, I'd jump with you. How else do you think you'd survive the swim? I was made for this. Mermaid, remember?" I winked and moved out of his arms so I could go change.

He waited in the office while I cleaned up with a wash bucket and towel. I moved to slip the light gray dress Lia gave me on, but I hissed in pain as it grazed my wound.

Adrian came through the doorway and moved to the side of the bed where I sat trying to catch my breath. I wasn't prepared for so little movement to take all my energy from me. The healing process was taking more out of me than I'd realized.

"Does it hurt?" he asked, his hand hovering over my wound's wrapping.

"Only when I touch it," I explained. "It's mostly healed thanks to my mom, but still painful."

He nodded and I glanced at his back, wondering if his own wounds were still bothering him.

"What about you?" I reached out and played with the hem of his tunic.

Smirking, he grabbed my hand and brought it to his lips. "You just want me to take off my shirt. I'm starting to think you only love me for my body."

Shrugging, I said, "It might be a part of it. Come on. I'm starving."

When we stepped outside of Jami's quarters, Lia was there to escort us to the galley. She walked at Adrian's side, and

I realized that she didn't trust him. Most likely *none* of my family did.

"That dress looks way better on your than it ever did on me," Lia said, reaching out and toying with the fluttering sleeve over my shoulder.

I turned back and said, "I doubt that."

Lia scoffed but said nothing else as we descended the stairs.

Adrian and I grabbed our bowls of food and joined Lia and Jami at a small wooden table.

"Where are my parents?" I asked. I hadn't seen them since they'd visited me in Jami's room.

"Bree is insisting on going with Nix, and your parents are busy trying to convince her otherwise. However, your sister is just as headstrong as you, if not more so, so you can imagine how that's going," Lia explained.

Adrian squeezed my knee under the table.

I grinned and said, "Well, we had to have gotten it from somewhere."

Jami laughed. "Oh, we know. I grew up with your father, and Lia with your mother, so we've seen how they can be. Bree will get her way, and Nix will keep her safe. I'm not worried about that."

Lia nudged him with her elbow. "*We* were never like that, though," she said.

Jami's lack of response said more than anything else could have.

"Captain, I'm surprised you're eating down here with the crew," Adrian said. "My father wouldn't be caught dead eating in the galley."

195

"You can call me Jami. I eat with my crew as often as I can, though I admit it's not as often as I'd like. Separating myself from them is no way to gain their trust or respect."

Adrian propped his elbow on the table and leaned his chin onto his hand. "I've found that fear is a powerful motivator, which is what my father tends to use."

I put my hand on Adrian's knee, squeezing. This wasn't the time to push buttons.

Jami studied Adrian. "Fear can be useful," he mused. "But I'd prefer if only people *outside* my crew feared me. Not that I'm vying for your father's title or anything. I'm happy to let him keep that one."

"Finn used it, for a while," Adrian said.

Lia glanced up and smiled at someone behind us.

"Ay, I did," Finn said, and I wanted to curl in on myself. He put his hands on my shoulders. "And I'd be happy to talk about it with you another time. Right now, we have something more pressing to discuss."

I turned to look at him. My mother stood beside him, worrying at her bottom lip.

"Where's Bree?" I asked.

"With Nix," Viv said. "And they are both going to be back safely by morning or else."

I didn't ask what the '*or else*' was, but I assumed it had to do with sending an army after her or something equally as dramatic. Not that I wouldn't be right there alongside that army.

"Let's go to my office," Jami said, pushing up from the table. "We can make our plans. I'd like Garrett to join us as well."

Finn nodded in agreement and said, "Of course."

196

"Who is Garrett?" Adrian asked.

"Jami's first mate," I explained. "It used to be Uncle Charles, but he decided to settle down in Sylvane a few years ago."

We stood to follow Jami and Finn, but Viv stopped me.

"Lia and I are going for a swim; do you want to see if the inhibitor wore off and join us?" she asked.

Adrian waited for me at the foot of the stairs. It seemed like a bad idea to leave him alone with my father and Jami for too long, but it could also be *good*.

"Sure." I waved to Adrian as he left.

Lia followed us to the main deck, where we took turns climbing down a rope secured to one of the masts, into the water. At first, when I tried to shift, nothing happened. Not even a tingle.

"I don't know," I said. "Nothing's happening."

"Give it a few seconds," Lia called. She was already farther out, while Viv remained by my side.

Closing my eyes, I tried to feel my shifter side. The magic of it, and the pull that I usually felt when near water.

A small tingle started in my feet, and then moved up my legs and my waist, and the next time I tried to shift, my tail appeared. I let out a cry of excitement. I hadn't realized how worried I'd been about it until the relief settled in.

"Thank Neros," I murmured. I could already feel my wound from the bullet healing more rapidly as the aching eased.

Viv grinned and squeezed my hand before diving down and joining Lia. Beneath the water, life always seemed a little less complicated. I could pretend that no one was after me, and Marley wasn't currently in my place in Captain Kerrigan's brig.

197

Adrian

"You know the layout of the ship," Jami said to me.

"It's much like yours. The galley and crew's quarters are swapped, but otherwise it's the same," I said, lifting my hands in a shrug, the shackles that had been replaced on my wrists restricting me. "Marley is most likely being kept in the captain's quarters. After Nora's escape, he won't keep her in the brig."

Finn and Jami stood on the other side of a long, rectangular table. Garrett sat next to me, his feet propped on the table as he stared at it, deep in thought. Or he could just be bored.

I continued. "Our best bet would be to lure both my father and Morgan off the ship. They'll leave someone to watch her, but they'll be nowhere near as lethal as Morgan."

"What's her deal?" Garrett asked, speaking up for the first time. "She's your father's first mate, but how did she get that role?"

A story I'd only ever heard from Polly. Morgan had been my father's first mate since his original one had been killed by a mermaid. One I now knew to be Lia. Apparently, a common need for revenge is what brought Morgan and my

198

father together. I'd no idea what revenge they sought, since neither of them spoke much about it. It was around that time that my father lost the last shred of whatever human decency he had left, according to Polly.

"Morgan's equally as vicious and cruel as my father. She and I were the ones who would keep everyone in line, and we'd dole out the punishments. She taught me everything I know." Looking down at my hands, I wondered what she would say, knowing I was *choosing* to stay in the shackles.

"So, you think you could take her down?" Garrett removed his boots from the table and leaned toward me, resting his forearms on his knees. "Because otherwise, why are you here?"

I expected either Jami or Finn to chime in, but they both looked expectant, waiting for my answer.

I moved my gaze slowly between each of them. "Morgan has hinted in the past that she's a shifter, but I've never seen her shift and I don't have any idea what kind of shifter she might be. If it were just her and I, without either of us shifting, then yes. I could take her."

"What kind of shifter are you?" he continued the questioning. I'd been expecting it from Finn, or even Jami, but not him.

Instead of answering, I protracted my fangs and bared them.

"That could come in handy," Jami commented. "How fast does your venom work?"

I retracted my fangs and shrugged. "Depends on their size. Someone Morgan's size would start to feel the effects of the venom almost immediately. It's a searing pain and then slowly

ebbs until your entire body goes numb. Finally, if you don't get an antidote within twenty minutes, it's lethal."

"What about for someone Kerrigan's size?" Finn asked.

"You want me to kill my own father?" I asked. It was something I'd imagined a thousand times, but never truly considered.

"If it comes down to it." Finn put his hands on the table and leaned in. "Kerrigan wants to sell my daughter to someone who will keep her in a cage, refusing to let her shift unless prompted, and experiment on her until all joy and hope has been leeched from her." The rage burning in Finn's eyes mirrored how I felt thinking of Nora being treated that way.

"I will kill my father, and any other person who threatens to take Nora, to keep her from that fate," I ground out, meaning every word.

Garrett drummed his fingers on the table and nodded to my shackles. "You can easily get out of those by shifting," he pointed out.

I leaned back in my chair and smirked, twisting my wrists. "I could. If I wanted."

Finn pinched the bridge of his nose and waved a hand at Garrett. "Take them off."

Leaning forward, Garrett pulled a set of keys from his pocket and unlocked the shackles, letting them fall to the floor. I rubbed my wrists where they were sore from the rubbing of the metal.

Finn straightened and nodded. "Now, let's get these plans nailed down."

Hours later, I emerged from Jami's quarters and, like on my father's ship, there was a table set up where some of the crew were playing cards.

"I thought I was going to have to come in after you," Nora said, coming up behind me, her smiling taking the weight from my shoulders.

I slipped my hand into hers, squeezing it tightly.

"Did you all figure out how we're going to save Marley?" Her brow furrowed in worry, and I wanted to reach out and smooth it for her. It hurt to know someone she loved was in danger and there was nothing I could do to ensure their safety.

"I think so. There are a few variables that might throw us off, but nothing we can't handle," I said, toying with the end of her braid.

She pursed her lips and put her hand over mine, stilling its movements. "What's bothering you?" she asked.

I blinked in surprise. I thought I'd been hiding my discomfort well, but apparently not.

"It's nothing. Just tired," I lied. Finn had been smart enough to ask me whether I could kill my father, but he hadn't pressed me much on Morgan. If it came down to killing the two of them, Morgan would be the more difficult of the two, and not because of her strength or possible shifter abilities.

Morgan had practically raised me, and she was the closest thing I had to a guardian in this world. We may not trust each other, or even like each other, but she was always the one who showed up to take me back to the ship after I fought my battles.

Something Morgan said to me the first time I'd been captured in an attempt to blackmail my father, and she showed

up to walk with me back to the ship, came back to me. Words that at the time, I'd brushed off, but now I reconsidered them.

"If you're going to be stupid, you're going to need to learn to defend yourself. No one else if going to save you, and I'm not ready to send you six feet under." It was the only time she looked at me with something like concern in her gaze. I couldn't help but think she did care about me, whether she knew how to show it or not.

But if it came down to choosing between Nora and Morgan, I'd make the call, no hesitation. Nora would come before anyone else, always.

Nora didn't look like she believed me that I was only tired, but she didn't call me out on my lie. We moved to stand at the side of the ship, away from everyone else.

"Unfortunately, we don't get our own room on this ship. We have to sleep in hammocks with the rest of the crew," she said.

"Mm. I think I'll survive a few nights in a hammock."

"Well, you *did* spend two nights on the floor avoiding me, so a hammock is no big deal" she said, poking me in the chest.

"I don't know who that was, but it couldn't have been me. I'd never give up a night alone with you." I wrapped my arms around her waist.

"Mmhmm." She leaned into me, resting her head against my chest.

Somehow, sleeping in a hammock was worse than sleeping on the floor. It had been so long since I'd had to sleep in one, I'd forgotten how atrocious they were. Anytime I rolled

in my sleep, I'd nearly fall out of the hammock and wake myself up. Not to mention how constricting the whole thing was.

Nora ended up with the privilege of staying with her mother in the first mate's cabin while he took a hammock. I was fast finding out how different things were on this ship than on the *Wave Breaker.*

Before most of the crew woke, I headed up to the main deck, unable to sleep another second in the hammock. I was surprised to find Finn already awake, gazing out over the railing on the starboard side of the ship. I considered going back downstairs, but he saw me and jerked his head for me to join him.

"Did you sleep?" I asked when I got close enough to see the bags under his eyes.

"Not at all," he said. "My daughter is out there right now; I won't sleep until she returns."

"Weren't they supposed to return this morning?"

He didn't respond.

We stood side by side, arms resting on the railing, as we watched the waves. At first, I thought maybe he was silently judging me, but then I realized, he was just intently watching for Bree.

A hawk landed to my right and at first, I thought it was Marley somehow. But then it shifted, and Garrett stood there, thankfully fully clothed. My clothes were also magicked to shift with me.

"I spotted Nix and Bree," he announced. "They should be back any minute. I'll lower the rope for them."

"Thank you, Garrett," Finn said. His features became less pinched, and the relief was almost palpable. "I'll go tell Viv and Nora."

I made myself scarce while Nix and Bree were pulled back onto the ship. Nix wouldn't want to see me, and I didn't particularly want to hear about how Marley was faring, in case it wasn't good. Marley had told me to get Nora out, and I had, but I couldn't help but feel partially responsible for her being taken captive.

Nix didn't come looking for me to kill me, so I had to assume Marley was still alive at least.

After a while, I felt like I could slip into the ocean, and no one would even notice. Nora spent the day with her sister, which I couldn't fault her for, but it was a little slap of reality.

When we'd been on Kerrigan's ship, I'd had the false sense that Nora *needed* me, at the very least to keep her safe, and now, that feeling was gone. She had her entire family and then some looking out for her and wanting her time and attention.

I'd never had anything like that. Polly was probably the only one other than my father and Morgan who had noticed my absence on the *Wave Breaker*.

It turned out that the rum was kept in the same place on this ship as it was on my father's ship. It worked equally as well to drown out my thoughts, too. Old habits died hard.

I stayed down in the cargo hold, laying on my back on the floor, with one leg bent.

At some point, Nix showed up, and I expected her to yell at me or maybe even try to kill me. But instead, she took the

bottle from me and drank from it, dropping down on the floor beside me, and letting out a long sigh.

"What's it like?" she asked. This was the first time we'd really spoken, other than when we'd been in the water.

"What's what like?"

"Being the one who won't live as long as the person you love." Her eyes flicked to me. "I *assume* you love Nora or else you wouldn't be here."

She assumed correct. "I hadn't thought about it. Why?"

"I never considered what it may be like to find someone you love so much you'd give up hundreds of years of life for them rather than live without them for a single day." She stared at the planks above us, never turning her gaze to me.

"Oh? And what's it like?" I asked.

"Every day feels like it has to matter. Marley has so many less days than I do, and each year we get closer to when she'll leave me alone to navigate this stupid world. Not having her here with me now, it feels like I'm missing a limb." She lifted an arm and dropped it. "I'd *rather* be missing a limb."

I wondered if that would be how Nora felt someday. As a mermaid, she'd live hundreds of years longer than I would. It was why mermaids often paired with other mer shifters. So they'd never have to go through what Nix was experiencing.

"Why are you down here?" she asked, turning her head to look at me.

I met her gaze. "Was Nora looking for me?"

"No." She handed me the bottle. "You know, this won't be what it's like every day. Her family won't always be around."

"I know." I leaned up so I could take a swig of rum.

"Marley and I have been traveling the world for years. But it's always nice to have a place where we can stop and stay for a while. Finn and Viv's home has been that place for all of us, and it can be that for you and Nora, if you decide to stay together."

If. Nix was the first one who talked as if we didn't have to make that decision right now. If we lived in a perfect world, and there was no one out to get either of us, then I'd say there was no question. Nora was *mine.*

But we didn't live in a perfect world.

"I don't blame you for Marley winding up on your father's ship, you know," Nix said. "She may not always show she cares, but she'll be the first to run into a dangerous situation for any of our family members or friends."

"I'm sure Finn told you we have a plan to get her back safely," I said.

Sighing, Nix said, "Yes. He did. I argued that not knowing what kind of shifter Morgan is will be too much of a wild card, but Finn thinks he can handle her."

"You don't think he can?" I had faith in Finn and believed he could win in a fight against Morgan, but Morgan fought dirty. She wouldn't make it easy.

"I think Finn still thinks he's twenty-six years old and able to fight twenty men off at once. But, if he believes he can do it, I won't question him."

Nix and I laid there for a while, passing the bottle back and forth. She told me a few stories from when she first met Marley and the pirates, and I shared a few of my own from the times I'd been captured and fought my way out.

Eventually, we had to return to the main deck before people went searching for us. I tried to convince Nix no one would be looking for *me,* but she countered that as a possible threat, I'd be missed. I conceded she was probably right.

"There you are!" Nora said as soon as she saw us. When she was at my side, she took my hand and said quietly, "I thought you might have actually jumped ship, and I'd have to go after you."

"I had my eye on him," Nix said, overhearing.

Nora wrinkled her nose. "Have you two been drinking? You smell like rum."

"And that's my cue, have a nice night." Nix strode away, heading for the card table and taking a seat beside Garrett.

"We may have had a drink or two," I said, leaning against the side of the ship so I wouldn't sway with its movements. I didn't often drink enough to feel drunk, but I could at least confirm that I was buzzed.

A breeze swept across the deck, making the hair not tamed within Nora's braid dance around her face. I reached out and tucked a few hairs behind her ear, just for an excuse to touch her.

"I guess I should be happy that you and Nix are getting along now," she said, her gaze flicking to Nix. "She and Marley both mean a lot to me." Looking down, she clasped her hands and toyed with a ring she wore on her index finger. I hadn't seen it before, which meant it was new. It also reminded me that I'd yet to give her a ring, even though we were technically married.

"Who gave you that?" I asked, gently taking her hands in mine and brushing my thumb over the ring. The deep blue coloring of it reminded me of the sea.

"It's Bree's. I have a matching necklace, but it's back home. Bree gave me her ring to hold onto when she went with Nix, and I guess I didn't really want to return it yet." She laughed. "It makes me feel closer to her, even though we don't get to spend as much time together lately."

"I should have got you a ring when we were in Lanteria," I said.

She furrowed her brow. "Why?" And then realization washed over her face. "Oh." Her cheeks turned bright red.

Leaning in and lowering my voice to a purr I asked, "Did you already forget you're my *wife?*" I bit my lip and leaned back enough so that I could see the look in her eyes. The *desire* that burned there, reflecting my own desire for her.

She ran her tongue over her bottom lip, her eyes glued to my mouth.

"Am I interrupting something?" Finn came up beside me.

I'd heard his approach and didn't flinch or take my eyes from Nora, who startled and looked as if she'd been caught in bed with me rather than simply standing on the deck.

"Just talking with my—"

"Nothing!" Nora spoke over me. Her smile was too big and her eyes too wide to appear casual.

Finn gripped my shoulder a bit too hard. "You should join the card game," he said.

I glanced over at him, but Nora spoke first.

"We'll be over in a minute," she said.

When Finn had gone, she turned her face back to me and whispered, "I haven't told them yet."

208

It didn't surprise me, but unexpectedly, it did sting. "Are you ashamed to be my wife, Nora?" I asked, trying to sound light and teasing.

"No!" She gripped my hand. "No, I'm not ashamed. I told you I loved you and I meant it. Do you believe me?"

"No one's ever loved me before, so I find it hard to *believe* you, but I trust you." I'd spilled more truth than I'd meant to, and I blamed the rum.

Nora cupped my face in her hands. "I love you, even if you can't say it back right now. I'll show you what love is." She kissed me and turned away, taking my hand and pulling me behind her as she walked to the card table.

Nora

Garrett was sent to deliver a message to Captain Kerrigan, letting him know where Finn and Jami would be waiting for him to make an exchange for Marley. Nix and Garrett would go to Kerrigan's ship once Morgan and Captain Kerrigan debarked to retrieve Marley, assuming they left her behind.

When we docked in Asmara, disappointment prickled at me. It was strange, thinking about everything that had happened since we'd left, and in such a short time. Stepping off the ship onto the docks made it feel like it had all been a dream.

Adrian had debarked earlier, with my father and Jami. Without him by my side it was all too easy to convince myself that he'd been a figment of my imagination.

"Nora," Bree called my name as she hurried down the gangplank, jumping at the end and landing beside me. "I'm coming with you." She looped her arm around mine. Her light blue dress was like the one I wore. They had belonged to Lia and were both magicked to shift with us.

210

Resting my head on her shoulder, I sighed, and we started our walk down the dock, toward the inn where we'd be staying until Kerrigan had been taken care of.

"Can you promise if I tell you something that you won't tell mom and dad?" I asked.

"Of course! You can tell me anything, and I promise I won't tell anyone, *especially* mom and dad." Bree squeezed my arm.

Lifting my head, I leaned in closer so no one would overhear, not that anyone we knew was close enough to.

"Captain Kerrigan married Adrian and I," I admitted, warmth filling me.

"What?!" Bree stopped and gaped at me. "Nora!"

"Shh!" I swatted at her and dragged her along so we wouldn't draw attention.

She dipped her head and lowered her voice. "You're married, Nor! And I wasn't there ..."

"If I'd had a choice in venue, trust me I would have ensured it was somewhere you could attend. However, Captain Kerrigan didn't give us much choice," I explained.

"Well." Bree sighed. "The least you can do is give me a play by play of your time on the ship once we're in our room."

We passed stalls of different merchants, selling clothing, food, jewels, and other wares. On a normal day, Bree and I would have stopped at all of them, but we had our orders to go straight to the inn and lock ourselves away. As if that would protect us if someone truly meant us harm. But, if it would give those fighting some peace of mind, we'd do it without too much complaint.

The Flightdeck Inn was at the top of a steep hill, and by the time we reached it, Bree and I were both winded.

"I need to work on my cardio outside of the water," Bree said, laughing. "I swear, I never get winded like this when I'm swimming."

Lia caught up with us and opened the front door, waving inside. "Your mother and I will be in the dining room if you need us. We'll send some food up to you two."

Viv had lagged, keeping an eye out for anyone following us.

"Make sure to grab a couple cinnamon buns please!" Bree said and skipped into the foyer of the inn.

I followed, much more melancholy. Bree always had the ability to be so cheerful, even in dire situations such as the one we were in. Not that I had any doubt that my family would win a fight against Captain Kerrigan and his crew.

"Room two eighteen!" Lia called up the stairs after Bree.

I laughed, waving to Lia as I headed to the room. The door was open when I arrived. Bree had already gone inside, but it was dark, which seemed odd.

"Bree, why do you insist on trying to fumble around in the—" I flicked on the lights and gasped.

"Any sudden moves or attempts to call for help, and your sister dies," Morgan said, unaffected, as usual. She had one hand clamped over Bree's mouth and the other holding a knife to her throat. Blood trickled down Bree's neck and my blood boiled at the sight of it.

My entire body shuddered as if preparing to shift, but I fought it, knowing that to shift would mean Bree's death.

"We thought we'd give you a warm welcome upon arrival, *daughter,*" Captain Kerrigan drawled from where he sat in an oversized armchair in the opposite corner to Morgan. The bed was between them, and I tried to come up with some way I'd be able to use that to my advantage, but there was no scenario in which I could save Bree before Morgan killed her. "Little did I know that there were *two* of you." His eyes darted to Bree before returning to me.

Lifting my hands, I looked at Captain Kerrigan. "What do you want?"

"Close the door," he commanded. Once I'd done that, he stood. "Now, the two of you are coming with us."

"Where's Marley? What did you do to her?" I asked, my hands shaking as I kept them up.

Morgan moved toward the wall with Bree firmly in her grip.

Captain Kerrigan stepped around the bed, grabbing my arm and pulling me toward Morgan. "What makes you think I did anything to her? Maybe she works for me now."

I bit my cheek so I wouldn't laugh. Instead, I scoffed. "She would never."

A twinge in my side made me curse, and I looked down to see Captain Kerrigan pulling a syringe back. "So you don't get any ideas."

The shifter suppressant washed over me, and I slumped against Captain Kerrigan. As revolting as he was, I couldn't bring myself to move.

Pressing her back against the wall, Morgan grunted from the effort, but a soft *click* preceded the wall opening to a dark tunnel.

"What ..." I gaped at the hole.

"You learn a lot when you make a living for yourself in the underside of the world," Captain Kerrigan said, yanking me toward the passageway where Morgan and Bree had disappeared. I stumbled alongside him. "Your father probably knew of these passages once, but it's been so long since he's even cared about this life that they slipped from his mind." He tugged on my arm again.

In the tunnel, there were no lights and when the wall closed behind us, we were left in pitch darkness.

"My father was never as horrible as you," I said.

"You know nothing of what your father has done." Captain Kerrigan's voice was right in my ear, low and threatening. I pulled away instinctively, but his grip on my arm kept me from escaping.

We kept moving through the hidden passageway. There were small slivers of light here and there where the boards of the walls weren't quite lined up. A set of stairs brought us to the first level, but then we went down another set, and entered a dirt tunnel. We were no longer in the inn, but underground.

"When my mother and Aunt Lia realize we're missing, they'll come for us," I said. "They took down the siren queen, in case you forgot. So, something tells me *you* won't be able to best them."

Captain Kerrigan's laugh echoed down the tunnel.

Occasionally, grunts came from ahead of us, but I couldn't be sure if it was Bree or Morgan. The tunnel started to take us upwards, and we entered a small cave that emptied out into the middle of a forest. With the shifter suppressant coursing through me, nothing seemed as bright or as lively as it should.

The way Bree moved, sluggish and uncoordinated, told me that Morgan must have used the shifter suppressant on her too. Something was different about this dose, almost like it was stronger. The first time hadn't left me quite so ... useless.

Clouds had rolled in since we'd gone inside, as if they knew something sinister was taking place below. The trees blocked most of the rain drops, but a few found their way to us. Normally in the rain, my mer-form would yearn to be unleashed, pushing me to shift, but I could no longer feel that side of myself.

"Morgan, you stay here with the girl," Captain Kerrigan said. "You know what to do if I'm not back here in half an hour."

Morgan nodded.

My eyes widened in panic. "You can't hurt her," I gasped, my mind reeling. "She's a dual shifter like me! She's worth more to you alive." I wasn't sure if she would present with dual shifting abilities yet, but I had to try to get through to Captain Kerrigan somehow.

Turning his head to me slowly, he curled his lip. "My revenge is worth more to me than any amount of gold. Besides, you'll fetch me enough of a price to keep my crew happy."

I deflated.

Yanking on my arm, Captain Kerrigan got us moving again. I didn't have enough strength to fight against him even if I wanted to. I'd never put Bree in danger, and I'd do whatever it took to ensure Morgan didn't hurt her any more than she already had.

Glancing at Bree one last time, I tried to give her a nod to let her know I'd be back for her, but even that seemed like

215

too much effort with the suppressant wreaking havoc. Her jaw was set, and her gaze hard, and I knew she wouldn't go down without a fight. Neither would I.

Captain Kerrigan led me through the trees, his arm around my shoulders the only thing keeping me standing.

"We should be close," he said.

"Kerrigan!" Finn's voice boomed through the forest. "I know you're here."

Instead of feeling relief, fear gripped me. If my father killed Captain Kerrigan, then that meant Morgan would kill Bree if we couldn't get back to them in time.

"Let me go ahead and warn them not to hurt you," I pleaded with Captain Kerrigan. "I promise I won't try to run."

"I've been scorned by your family one too many times to trust your word. No. You'll stay with me." He shoved me in front of him, no longer supporting me.

Stumbling, I tried my best to stay upright. Captain Kerrigan was only a few steps behind me as I made my way through the underbrush. Thank the gods I wasn't trying to be stealthy because anyone within a mile radius would hear me coming.

When I cleared a few more trees and bushes, I caught sight of the group who had left the ship that morning with my father. My legs gave out and I dropped to my hands and knees, gasping from the exertion.

"Nora!" Adrian cried. "What are you—"

"Don't move, son," Captain Kerrigan snarled, stepping into view beside me and kicking my boot.

"If you touch my daughter again, I will tear you limb from limb," Finn growled.

216

I couldn't tell where everyone was, or if they had moved, because my head was too heavy to lift, and I could barely focus as I tried my hardest to fight against the shifter suppressant.

Captain Kerrigan guffawed. "*Your* daughter, Finn? You must not have heard the news. She's *our* daughter now, and I promise to treat her like my own." Nudging me with his foot, I fell onto my side. It didn't take much, and I didn't fight it.

Staring up at the sky, I watched the rain slide down the leaves and counted the drips that landed on me.

"What are you ..." Finn trailed off. Even though I couldn't see them, I could imagine Finn had turned on Adrian, probably as Captain Kerrigan had planned. "You married my daughter? I'll kill you."

"Enough," Jami said. "You can kill *him* later. Right now, we need to deal with Kerrigan."

"Right." Finn huffed. "What do you want?"

Leaning my head back, I saw them all, upside down. Adrian was the closest to me, while Finn and Jami were across the small clearing.

"First and foremost, I want my son dead," Captain Kerrigan drawled. "You can thank me for that one later, Finnian."

"With pleasure," Finn growled.

With what little strength I had I flipped over so the world would no longer be upside down, and got to my knees, yelling, "Don't kill him!"

Everyone stopped moving.

"Yes. Don't kill him." Captain Kerrigan gripped my arm and yanked me to my feet. "I'm saving that for Nora."

"What? No!" I fought against him with everything, but it wasn't nearly enough. Some of my strength was returning, but I wouldn't be back to myself fully for at least a couple hours.

"Remember what happens to your sister if you don't do as I say," Captain Kerrigan whispered low in my ear so no one else would hear. "And if you so much as *hint* that she's my leverage, she dies."

Dragging me toward Adrian, the captain pulled a dagger from a sheath at his side and pressed it into my hand.

Adrian didn't move. He stared at me, unblinking and unafraid. He probably assumed I'd never even consider killing him.

Tears streamed down my face, mixing with the raindrops as they fell more steadily. The world had been blurry before, but now we may as well be underwater with sand kicking up around us.

"I'll give you a second to say your goodbyes," Captain Kerrigan said, releasing my arm and giving me a push toward Adrian.

I stumbled into him, my hands pressed against his chest and his arms came around me, keeping me from falling.

"Are you alright?" Adrian asked.

I shook my head and leaned my forehead against him.

"Of course not, stupid question." His arms tightened on me. "Don't worry, I'll get you out of here."

Captain Kerrigan cleared his throat. "Times up, dear Nora! Kill him."

218

Adrian

Nora lifted her head, tears streaming down her cheeks. "I'm so sorry," she said, sobs cracking her voice.

I didn't understand what she meant until her hand that held the dagger lifted. Her arm shook with the effort and her sobs told me that something more was going on here. So, I didn't fight her or move away. If killing me was what she needed to do, then I'd gladly die for her.

"Tick tock, Nora," Captain Kerrigan said. He was in reach, but I worried if I tried to go for him, whatever had Nora convinced she needed to kill me would come to pass. I knew my father and he wouldn't have come here without contingencies in place.

Placing my hand under Nora's elbow, I helped support her as she placed the dagger's tip against my chest, right over my heart.

"It would be easier to aim for the jugular," I pointed out, unable to stop myself from smiling at her.

"Nora, stop this," Finn said, moving toward us.

Captain Kerrigan put his hand up and took a step closer to Nora, saying, "You're going to want to let this happen."

"It's okay, Nora," I said, ignoring the argument between Finn and my father.

She shook her head, her eyes clenched shut.

I brushed my thumb along her jaw and lifted her face to mine. When she opened her eyes, she gasped and kissed me.

"I love you," she said. "Even if you can't say it back." She laughed through her sobs.

Pressing my forehead to hers, I closed my eyes and said, "I love you, too, Nora."

She inhaled sharply and the dagger dropped from her hand, landing softly between us in the grass.

The bushes rustled from the direction Kerrigan and Nora had come from and Lia emerged, pulling someone behind her.

Morgan.

"Found her," Lia said, shoving Morgan to her knees. "I noticed the girls were missing from their room, so Viv and I came out looking for them. We split up, and I found Morgan."

Even at her enemy's mercy, Morgan still showed no sign of distress or uncertainty. Neither did my father, and that scared me more than anything else ever had.

Nora turned away from me, stumbling, but I caught her.

"Where's Bree?" she asked.

I could have sworn the ghost of a smile crossed Morgan's face, but she remained staring ahead, not saying anything.

"What do you mean?" Lia asked. "Bree wasn't with her."

Nora pulled away from me with more strength than I thought she had since she'd clearly been given a shifter inhibitor, and crossed the clearing, dropping to her knees in front of Morgan and gripping the front of her shirt.

"What the fuck did you do to my sister?"

I was about to go to her, when my father pulled out his pistol and pointed it at me, cocking it.

"Let her go, Nora," Kerrigan said. "Or else I'll finish what you couldn't." Turning back to me he added, "And if you shift or try to run, Nora will take your bullet."

My snake fangs snapped out as if in protest.

Kerrigan smirked and moved closer, pressing the gun against my forehead. "I've been considering doing this for a while now. Your usefulness has finally been outweighed by my ire."

Another gun cocked to my left, but I kept my stare pinned on my father.

"I think you're forgetting who has the upper hand here," Jami said.

"No one move!" Nora cried. "We don't have the upper hand."

My gaze flicked to her where she still knelt in front of Morgan, her hands at her sides.

"It's alright, darling," Kerrigan said, turning to look at Nora over his shoulder. "You can tell them. She's in a secure location where they'll never find her."

"What ... Who is he talking about, Nora?" Finn asked.

"If it's Marley, she can take care of herself," Lia said, though her throat bobbed.

Nora shook her head. "Not Marley. It's Bree. They have Bree."

Finn shifted into his lion form, as if he'd lost control. I could understand. If something were to happen to Nora, I imagined I'd react similarly.

"Dad, don't!" Nora got to her feet, a little less shaky than before, and put her hands out toward him. "They'll kill her."

A growl reverberated through the small clearing and Finn bared his teeth, kneading the ground with his claws. I could understand how he'd once been the most fearsome pirate before my father.

After a few tense seconds, Finn shifted back into his human form, his clothes shifting with him. "Lia, Jami, go find Bree and Viv," he demanded. Neither of them moved until Finn said, "Now."

Once Lia and Jami were gone, Morgan rose from the ground but remained where she was beside Nora.

"I've been waiting for this moment for a *long* time, Finn," Morgan said, her eyes blazing. It was more emotion than I'd ever seen from her.

Turning my attention back to Kerrigan, I asked, "Why do all this? Just to get Nora? To get your *revenge*?" He had never once been completely honest with me, so I don't know why I expected it now, but from the gleam in his eyes, I had a feeling he was in the mood to share his motivations.

"Nora is simply icing on the cake," Kerrigan said.

Morgan stalked toward Finn, no weapons in hand, but a wicked grin on her face.

"I bet you have no idea who I am," she said.

"Morgan." I tried getting her attention. "Stop this." If she had any care for me, I hoped that she might listen, but she didn't even turn her gaze my way.

Kerrigan backed away from me, not lowering his weapon that was still pointed at me.

"What are you talking about?" Finn asked, not moving as Morgan drew closer to him. "You're Kerrigan's first mate. You've caused almost as much pain as he has, if not more."

Morgan scoffed. "What I've done is nothing compared to what *you* did."

Kerrigan reached Nora, pulling her up from the ground with her arm and started tugging her toward the trees.

"What are you doing?" I yelled, taking a few steps forward before he pointed the gun at Nora instead of me, and I stopped, terror lancing through me.

Nora didn't budge, her eyes glued to Morgan and Finn.

"Brom thought that he was safe, never having relations with any other non-shifters," Morgan started, and my blood ran cold as I guessed where her spiel was headed. "Well guess what? My mother lied to him. She was so enthralled by him and his pirate ways; she lied and told him she was a shifter."

Finn's expression remained hard and unreadable, but I could *feel* the tension thickening in the air. It was only a matter of time before it burst.

"Of course, my mother didn't live through childbirth like yours did. She gave *everything* she had to me. She must have known I'd need it someday." Morgan's body seemed to ripple, and Finn cringed.

"You're my ..." he started to say, but he couldn't seem to get the words out.

223

"Sister? Well, half, but yes. And I'm here to kill you." Her eyes widened along with her grin.

Finn grimaced. "But, why?"

"You're the reason our father is dead, and I'll never meet him. He didn't deserve to go out the way he did. It should have been *Viv* on that ship when it blew."

That was all it took, and Finn's lion form took over as he shifted in a flash. Morgan laughed heartily before she too shifted.

Morgan's lioness form was as big as Finn's lion form, and equally as formidable. I'd promised that I'd help take her out if it came down to it, but looking at her in her shifted form, I wasn't so sure my venom would be enough to do the trick anymore.

Morgan leapt at Finn, tackling him to the ground.

"No!" Nora cried. Kerrigan still hadn't been able to get her away from the scene as he was clearly trying to. "Let me go!" She thrashed against Kerrigan, and just as her father's shift had seemed to explode over him, hers did too. One second, she was in Kerrigan's clutches, the next she was racing toward the fight in her lioness form.

I paused, admiring her for a few short seconds. She was magnificent, and the idea of anyone trying to cage her as my father intended was unfathomable.

As Kerrigan aimed his gun at Finn and fired a shot, I tackled him to the ground, sending the bullet wide. I struggled to get the pistol from him, baring my fangs at him.

"What are you going to do, son? Kill me?" He grunted as my fist struck him across the face. Laughing, he spit out blood onto the grass and dropped the pistol.

Pinning one of his arms to the ground, I managed to say, "If that's what I have to do to keep Nora safe."

Kerrigan pulled a second pistol from his belt with his free hand and fired another shot, a loud roar told me he had struck *someone.* But I couldn't shift my focus to find out who.

"It's interesting. I never thought you capable of caring about another person other than yourself." Kerrigan scowled and leaned his head back against the ground almost as if giving up. "Gods know you've been out to ruin my life since the moment you were dumped on my ship by your mother."

Smirking, I said, "You're not entirely wrong." There was some lost time between then and when I'd decided my father would never love or accept me and I set out to make his life as difficult as he'd made mine. But I'd learned a long time ago, there was no point arguing with Kerrigan. In his mind, he was always right.

"And now I'll finally be able to strip you of the only thing you ever cared about, your life as a captain," I said.

Bringing his head up too fast for me to move, he slammed his forehead against mine. I cursed and lost my grip on him, but he stayed down.

"As if my crew would ever follow the likes of you. The one who caused them so much pain, time and again." He laughed.

"At whose behest, *father?*" I used the word like a curse. He'd never wanted the title, and he cringed any time I used it. "We all know whenever I delivered those lashings to the crew it was at *your* command. Or Morgan's. But I'd do it again if it meant keeping Nora safe from you and whoever you planned on selling her to."

225

"Killing me won't change anything. There are powers larger than me who have plans for your girl and her father." He let out a long breath. "You wouldn't kill your own father, anyway," he said. "You're too *weak*. Besides, Morgan would never forgive you, and I know how much you care about her opinion. More than you ever cared about mine."

Baring my fangs and leaning in closer, I said, "I may care what Morgan thinks of me, but I care more what *Nora* thinks. And I won't let her down again." Sinking my fangs into his shoulder, he cried out and slammed the butt of his pistol against my skull. It was too late, though. My venom was already coursing through his veins. He'd be in too much pain to run or get help, and then, he'd be dead.

Nora

Somehow, despite the shifter suppressant that shouldn't have worn off yet, I'd managed to shift. With the shift, it seemed to burn what remained of the suppressant away and my strength returned along with clarity in my mind.

Narrowing my focus on Morgan, I aimed for her as she fought with my father. I wasn't sure where one of them ended and the other began. Claws, teeth, and blood all mixed, making a deadly combination.

The rain came down steadily, matting my fur and making the grass slick. Finn wound up pinned beneath Morgan, her teeth bared as she was about to lunge for his throat. I took my opportunity to leap on top of her, digging my claws into her shoulders as deep as they would go.

Morgan roared and it was enough of a distraction that Finn was able to move and shake Morgan off him, sending me tumbling from her back. I hadn't quite been in my lioness form long enough to understand how my body moved efficiently.

Shaking my head, I got my bearings. Finn and Morgan were already back at it, but Finn had deep claw marks down his side. Blood flowed freely from his wounds.

No. I won't let Morgan win. I steeled myself.

Waiting for another opening, I got it as my father and Morgan reared back simultaneously and I threw myself at Morgan, tackling her into the bushes. A shot rang out behind us, and my father roared. I prayed he hadn't been gravely injured. Morgan and I rolled for longer than I'd anticipated because there was a slight hill that had been concealed by the undergrowth.

Morgan leaped to her feet first, but it didn't take me as long to right myself as it had the first time. It still gave her enough time to latch onto my back leg with her teeth and yank it out from under me.

Growling, I turned my body to try and claw her and make her let me go, but she hung on. The searing pain wasn't as potent in my lioness form as pain usually was in my human form. It must have had something to do with the faster healing.

Finn barreled through the undergrowth and down the hill, blood trailing behind him, and Morgan released me, returning her focus to him. She stalked forward and lunged at him at the same time he lunged for her. There was less blood leaking from his wounds, but they weren't healing fast enough. If Morgan delivered more blows like that, it wouldn't take long for him to lose too much blood and either lose consciousness, or worse.

I wouldn't let it come to that.

Someone cried out back in the clearing, but I couldn't tell if it had been Adrian.

228

Taking a few heaving breaths, I refocused on the fight in front of me. I stretched my back leg, making sure I could still use it fully. It hurt to move, but I still had a full range of motion.

This time, I went for Morgan's back leg as she had with me. If I could off balance her, Finn might be able to gain the upper hand.

She moved too quickly, though, and I barely nipped her. A low rumble in her throat made it sound like she was laughing at me. She probably would have been if she were in her human form.

Finn swatted at me, as if he were trying to get me to leave, but I wouldn't. We both could see where this would end if I left him to fight Morgan alone.

But there was something else I'd had in the pocket of my dress that if I shifted, should still be there, magic-willing, that could end this all. I'd have to time it perfectly or else Morgan would kill me.

Backing away, I tried to collect my thoughts and formulate a plan. Instead, I gave Morgan the space she needed to attack Finn head on again, her claws knocking his muzzle to the side and giving her the opening to latch her teeth around his throat.

No! I screamed in my mind as he fell to the ground and Morgan released him. She hovered over him, about to deliver the final, killing blow.

Shifting back into my human form, I gripped the needle I'd stolen from Kerrigan's pocket and ran straight for Morgan. She didn't even flinch when I flung myself on her and jammed the needle into her neck.

The one perk of Kerrigan having me so close to his side while we'd walked there had been finding that syringe filled with shifter suppressant.

There was a terrifying few seconds where I thought that the suppressant hadn't worked, and Morgan was about to kill my father and then me. But then she shifted beneath me and landed face down in the dirt, my legs on either side of her hips.

In a burst of energy, she flipped over, grabbing her dagger from where she had it sheathed on her leg and held it to my throat. I put my hands up in surrender.

"Please, you don't have to do this," I huffed, trying to catch my breath from all the fighting. Leaning back, the dagger was no longer at my throat, so she pointed at it my chest. "You won't have the energy to finish the job. Trust me."

Morgan's teeth were gritted and her chest heaved.

"You don't know what strength I possess," she hissed. "I *will* kill you."

Gripping her hand that held the dagger, I pried her fingers from the hilt and took it from her.

"No, Morgan, *I* will kill *you*." I pressed the dagger to her throat as she'd had it to mine. "Unless you tell me where my sister is."

Morgan closed her eyes, and I half thought she might tell me what I wanted to know.

"She's probably already suffocated to death by now. A little consolation for not killing *you*," she snarled, spitting in my face.

I wiped it away and was about to respond when she jammed her finger into the wound from her bite on my leg.

Crying out, I pushed a little harder on the dagger, and blood rolled down Morgan's neck.

Finn stirred beside us, but didn't wake. His chest still rose and fell, weakly but enough to let me know he was alive.

Morgan laughed and broke into a coughing fit, the dagger scraping even deeper. "Just kill me already. I'm not telling you anything."

I gripped the dagger tighter, considering doing as she asked. It wasn't that I didn't think she deserved to die, but I'd never killed anyone before. The only person I'd considered killing and probably would have done so happily was Gregor, but Marley had taken care of him for me.

"Are you *scared,* Nora?" Morgan whispered, her eyes widening. "What if I told you that if you don't kill me, I'll kill your entire family? Well, the rest of them anyway. Bree's already dead."

She was egging me on, and it was working.

Shaking my head, I tried to reason with her. "Why do you want me to kill you so badly? Death isn't the only answer here, and it isn't the only way to end a fight."

"You're wrong," she said. "The *only* way this will end is with one of us lying in a pool of our own blood. The question is, will it be me, or you?"

"Nora!" Adrian called and I turned my head to find him running toward us.

Morgan's hand wrapped around my wrist and somehow, she found the strength to flip me onto my back and we switched positions. Adrian pulled her off me, falling back, with her wrapped in his arms. She scrambled to free herself, but before she could I crawled over to them, dagger still in hand. Without

thinking too much about it, I brought the dagger up above my head and slammed it down in Morgan's chest.

"I'm not afraid of killing you," I said, even though my hands shook as I released the dagger.

Blood bloomed from the wound and Morgan gasped.

"You—chose—good—Adrian," she said, between each breath. As her eyes fluttered shut, a smile graced her lips.

Adrian stared down at Morgan, his arms still wrapped around her even though she was going nowhere.

I reached out, touching his arm, and he flinched.

"Are you okay?" I asked.

Shaking his head he cleared his throat and said, "Yeah, sorry." He gently moved Morgan from his arms to the ground and stood. Holding his hand out to me, he helped me up.

I cursed when I put weight on my injured leg. I'd almost forgotten about the wound.

"You're hurt," Adrian said, tilting his head to look at my leg. "We should wrap that."

"I'm not worried about me right now," I said, turning to my father who was still unconscious in his lion form. Thankfully his bleeding seemed to have slowed from all his wounds.

"Nora!"

I was surprised to hear my mother's voice. She came running through the bushes and practically threw herself at me, wrapping her arms around me.

Lia came jogging up behind her, with Jami at her side. I let out a sigh of relief when I saw Bree right behind them. Extricating myself from my mother, I ran to Bree and hugged her tight.

"Why are you all dirty?" I asked, noting the dirt smears all over her, and the chunks of it falling from her hair.

Tears welled in her eyes, and she leaned her head on my shoulder.

"We need to tend to Finn," Lia said "You go, Viv. We'll take care of him. I promise."

I turned and saw my mother crouching beside my father, her hand on his side. Nodding, she stood and joined me and Bree, putting her arms around us both.

"I am *never* letting either of you out of my sight again," she said, kissing the top of my head and then Bree's.

"What happened to Kerrigan?" Jami asked.

"He's dead," Adrian said, his jaw clenching. "Or will be, soon." Clearing his throat, he turned to me. "Nora, can I talk to you for a second?"

Letting Bree lean on Viv instead of myself, I followed Adrian away from the rest of the group.

"This ..." He waved a hand around. "Is all my fault. If I'd just let you leave that night in Asmara instead of asking you to come with us to Lanteria, none of this would have happened. You wouldn't have almost lost your sister, and your father."

I placed my hands on either side of his face and looked into his eyes. "None of this is your fault. Kerrigan and Morgan were going to come after me and my father one way or another."

Placing his hands over mine, he stroked my wrist with his thumb. "I can go. If you want to be alone with your family."

"I don't want you to go." I shook my head. "I need you here. I *want* you here. You are my family, *husband,*" I teased, but I meant every word.

Adrian smiled and leaned down to kiss me.

233

"Nora!" Viv called. "We're heading back to the inn, but I'm not leaving without you."

I grasped Adrian's hand. "We're ready. Let's go."

"I should take care of a few things," Adrian said, pulling back. His gaze flicked to Morgan's body and my stomach dropped.

How could I have forgotten that I'd just killed the woman who'd been the closest thing he'd had to family? And his father ...

"I'll help," Lia said, stepping up beside him.

Looking back and forth between Adrian and my mother, I bit my lip. Being there for Bree was important to me, but so was being there for Adrian. But I couldn't be there for them both at that moment.

"I'll stay with you, Adrian" I said, squeezing Bree's hand before returning to Adrian's side. "I'm sorry, mom, but I can't go with you right now."

"But Nora, your sister needs you," Viv said, tears brimming in her eyes.

Bree lifted her head from Viv's shoulder and cleared her throat. The dirt on her face was streaked from her tears. "I understand, Nora. I'll be okay. Go with Adrian."

"I'll keep her safe, Viv," Lia said. "We'll be back as soon as we can."

I was convinced that my mother was going to protest and try to make me go with them, but she didn't.

"I'm counting on you," Viv said to Lia. "Bring them home safe."

Once Viv and Bree were gone, Jami and Adrian started digging two holes to bury Morgan and Kerrigan's bodies. They

found a place a little more off the beaten path, and buried Kerrigan first.

I sat beside Morgan, staring at the dagger protruding from her chest while Jami wrapped my leg wound between burying bodies. He hadn't said anything about Adrian and I being married, but I feared he might. Lia and my mother were the only ones still in the dark, and I wasn't quite ready to deal with them finding out yet.

"You know, this reminds me a lot of something that happened to your mother," Lia said from behind me where she was wrapping my father's wounds. He was still in his lion form, and had woken up, but his eyes were closed. "She had to kill a siren to save a little boy's life, and while it might not seem like a hard decision because we were at war with the sirens at the time, it weighed on her."

Jami finished wrapping my leg and left me and Lia to talk, while he helped Adrian lift Morgan and took her away.

"I'm fine, Aunt Lia," I said, pulling my knees to my chest and resting my arms on them. *Aunt.* A word that could have applied to Morgan as well, technically. A strange sensation washed over me. Sadness mixed with betrayal. My own aunt had tried to kill me and my father. "I know I did the right thing."

"Mhm. That's what your mother said too. You don't need to confide in me, but you should confide in *someone.*" She rested her hand on my shoulder and leaned back so I could see her. "We all have our demons, Nora, but they're only dangerous to us if we keep them locked inside where they'll tear us apart."

"Duly noted."

235

I stood and waited for Adrian and Jami to return. When they did, Adrian came up behind me and wrapped his arms around my chest, kissing the top of my head.

"You did what you had to do," he said.

Jami and Lia helped my dad to his feet. He was still in his lion form and would have to stay that way until his wounds were healed enough that they wouldn't kill him in his human form. The expedited healing of shifters only worked in their shifted forms.

I leaned back into Adrian, gripping his arms that were still around me, and let the tears that were fighting to break free fall.

"We're going to try to get back to the inn," Lia said, one hand on my father's shoulder. "Are you two headed to Kerrigan's ship?"

Adrian shook his head. "I'm sure they know what's going on by now if Nix and Garrett were able to get Marley safely off the ship. They can wait a little longer to find out the captain is dead."

I glanced up at him. "But—"

"Your family needs you right now, so that's where we'll be. There are plenty of people on the ship who will make sure nothing too crazy happens in the meantime." He brushed his thumb along my jaw and kissed my temple.

"Are you sure? Because I don't mind going with you to the ship first." As much as I wanted to be with my family, I didn't want to take Adrian away from his duty and I'd already agreed to be there for him, no matter what.

"Come on," he said, dropping an arm to my waist and leading me toward the others. "We're going with your family."

I kissed his cheek and reminded him, "They're *your* family now too."

Back at the inn, Viv and Bree were curled up in bed, while Lia sat on the edge of the bed, rubbing Bree's back. Finn curled up on the floor, too big for the bed in his lion form.

Bree had cleaned up since I'd seen her, and her hair was damp, braided into a neat plait down her back. Jami and Adrian were in the dining room getting us food.

I sat beside Lia, and she put her arm around my shoulders. "Jami let something slip on our walk back here."

Viv perked up at that and Bree cracked an eye.

"And what was that?" I asked, knowing exactly what he'd let slip.

Lia tapped my knee. "You should be the one to announce it, I think," she whispered.

Finn growled from his spot on the floor but didn't move or open his eyes.

Sighing, I gave in. "Adrian and I were married by Captain Kerrigan." I held my breath, waiting for my mom's response.

Viv didn't move, Bree still tucked into her side, but she sucked in a deep breath and let it out slowly.

"Do you love him?" she asked, her gaze meeting mine.

Nodding, I smiled and said, "Yes. I do."

"Okay. You've proved your old enough to make your own decisions, and I trust you to have made the right one in this case."

Moving around Lia, I laid down beside my mother and she pulled me in close to her side opposite Bree.

237

"Can I get married now?" Bree asked, teasing. "I think I saw a really cute guy in town on our way here this morning."

I swatted at her across Viv and stuck my tongue out at her. "Adrian isn't some *random* guy from town. We met on my way to Asmara, actually," I began, and told them the entire story of how we truly met and fell in love.

By the time I finished, Adrian and Jami came back into the room bearing multiple plates of delicious looking food that smelled amazing.

"Finally," Finn said. "I'm starving."

Viv and I sat up at the same time, surprised to hear his voice. It was a relief to see him back in his human form.

Viv kissed Bree on the top of the head and slid off the bed, crossing the room and gently taking Finn into her arms. Even though she was careful, he flinched. Viv had been so calm the whole time; I hadn't realized how truly worried she must have been about him.

Their love for each other always made me smile.

"Nix, Garrett, and Marley are downstairs having a drink," Jami said. "As it turns out, Marley convinced some of Kerrigan's crew to release her while Kerrigan was gone, and she was playing cards with them when Nix arrived to *save* her."

Adrian chuckled. "Polly wouldn't have let her waste away in the brig once my father left."

There was longing in his voice that I was surprised to hear. Even though it had only been a few days since he'd been with his father's crew, he actually *missed* them.

Once we ate, I suggested Adrian and I head back to the *Wave Breaker*. Now that I knew Bree, Finn, and Marley were

okay, I was ready to check on my new friends: Charlie, Billy, Nate, and Polly.

Finn shook his head. "It would be better if—"

"Let her go," Viv said, putting her hand on Finn's chest.

"But ... Right." He cleared his throat and looked to the ceiling. "Be careful, and make sure you come see us before you decide to run away again."

Rolling my eyes and smirking, I said, "I didn't run away the first time. But don't worry, I promise to inform you of any decisions we make on where we go from here."

We stopped downstairs to check in with Nix and Marley. They were the only two in the bar area, each with a glass of rum in front of them that hadn't been touched.

"Marley?" I said to get her attention as we approached. "I'm so glad you're okay."

She grinned and wrapped me in a one-armed hug. "Was there ever any doubt I would be?"

"Not really, but it was weird not having you around," I said.

"I'm glad I was missed. Are you headed out?" She glanced behind me at Adrian. "I would have prepared a welcome-back party for you on the ship before I left if I'd known you were headed there." She winked and patted my arm.

"Thank you for always protecting me." I kissed her cheek. "I'll see you soon." I hugged Nix before returning to Adrian's side.

"I'll make sure she stays in one piece," Adrian said.

Rolling my eyes, I pulled him away, back toward the exit and a new sense of freedom.

239

Adrian

Polly, Nate, and Charlie were waiting at the top of the gang plank when Nora and I arrived. Polly hugged Nora tight while Charlie went on about how Polly had been keeping everyone in line since we'd been gone.

"You should have seen her; she had this crew hanging on her every word like Kerrigan never could. Stupid bastard." Charlie flicked her gaze to mine. "Too soon?"

I shrugged. My father's death didn't affect me nearly as much as I thought it might have. Morgan's death on the other hand ... I could still hear her final words, *You chose good, Adrian.*

Had she truly only ever wanted what was best for me? Or was she as heartless and ruthless as I'd always believed her to be? Now, I'd never know for sure.

"Captain Kerrigan brought his death upon himself," Polly said, gripping my arm. "You have nothing to be ashamed of or feel sorry for."

"I feel neither of those things," I said.

Nora leaned into me, putting her arm around my waist. Having her there meant more than she could ever know.

When she'd chosen to go with me rather than her family, I'd been shocked. No one had ever put me first before or cared enough to stand beside me. But she had.

"We need to choose a new captain," Charlie said. "And most of the crew are ready to vote, whenever you're ready."

"Who are we voting for?" I asked, unable to think of anyone who could fill my father's shoes so easily.

Furrowing her brow, Charlie said, "Well, you, for one." She shook her head as if I should have known that.

"Just because you think people don't like you doesn't mean they don't think you'll make a good captain," Nora said, nudging my side with her elbow. "I happen to think you'd make a *great* captain."

"I'll go collect the votes," Charlie said, slipping away.

"We'll await the results elsewhere," I said to the others, taking Nora's hand and pulling her with me toward the stairs leading to the upper deck.

"What's wrong? You don't want to wait with Polly and Nate? They'll both vote for you, I know it," Nora said.

"Nothing's wrong. I just can't stand there with everyone expecting something of me." I'd never wanted to be captain, never even *considered* it. I always imagined I'd be long gone before my father died, and then Morgan would take over.

At the stern of the ship, I looked out to the sea with Asmara at our backs.

Nora cupped my face in her hands, turning my head to look at her.

"Do you not want to be captain?" she asked. "Because you *do* have a choice in the matter."

241

Closing my eyes, I pictured what it would be like to be captain. To have an entire crew willing to do whatever I asked of them. To never worry about being left behind again.

"I don't know what I want," I admitted, reaching up and placing my hand over hers. "But as long as I have you, I'm willing to try being a captain for this crew. If that's what they want."

"And we've yet to live out my fantasy that has to do with this railing," Nora said, leaning back to let her hair fly out behind her in the breeze. She bit her lip, and I captured her mouth with mine, grinding my hips against her and pinning her to that railing.

"You know how to change my mind," I said, smirking.

Nora's hands trailed beneath my shirt, and down to my rock-hard bulge straining to be unleashed upon her. I groaned into her mouth.

"Adrian," Polly called. "Incoming." There was a teasing lilt to her voice, but I still wanted to strangle her for interrupting my moment with Nora.

"What is it?" I snapped, turning my head, but keeping Nora pinned between my arms against the railing.

"I thought you might care to know the vote was nearly unanimous. Congratulations, *Captain*. You can think about who you want as a first mate overnight and deliver the news tomorrow. In the meantime, don't have too much fun celebrating." She waved as she left us alone again, heading back down the stairs.

Nora squealed in delight. "I knew it. Let's go celebrate!" She gripped my biceps.

242

Tucking my mouth into the crook of her neck, I kissed her slowly. "I'm not done with you yet, sweetheart."

She inhaled sharply and her grip on me tightened. "Thank the gods," she said. "Or should I be thanking you, *Captain?*"

"Mmm," I mused. "I think I'm going to like this captain thing."

243

H.M. Huntress

About the Author

H. M. Huntress is a self-published author and content creator. She has been writing stories since grade school and is driven by the desire to share her writing with the world while encouraging others to do the same. All her books are currently available on Amazon. If you want to connect with her on social media, find her at the handle below!

TikTok & Instagram: @authorhmhuntress

I'd love if you left a review for *Beneath Venomous Sails* on Amazon, Goodreads, or social media!

Scan here for updates on future projects and events!

H.M. Huntress

Check out my other books!

Haunting Memories

The Broken Angel Series:

Broken Angel
Condemned Angel
Forsaken Angel

The Unbound Series:

Unbound
Disgraced
Awakened

The Forbidden Waves Series:

Forbidden Waves
Ruthless Tides

Beneath Venomous Sails